FINE

John Patrick Higgins

© 2024 by John Patrick Higgins

All Rights Reserved.

Set in Mrs Eaves with LaTeX.

ISBN: 978-1-963846-02-7 (paperback)
ISBN: 978-1-963846-03-4 (ebook)
Library of Congress Control Number: 2024939895

Sagging Meniscus Press
Montclair, New Jersey
saggingmeniscus.com

*To Kelly Mullan Higgins,
who would have kicked her shoes across the room reading this book.*

If at first you don't succeed, failure may be your style.
—*Quentin Crisp*

Contents

Cafés of Desire	1
The Sound of Young People	6
And This Is Me …	13
The Pint of No Return	20
Summertime Special	31
Café de Flaw	40
The Playlist of the Gods	47
Through a glass, Barclays	54
It's the Most Wonderful Time of the Year	62
Fanfare for the Gammon Man	68
Spruces Rough in the Distant Glitter	75
I Know You're a Seasonal Beast	82
Silvia	89
Nite Flights	96
Alone and Palely Loitering	102
The Body in the Library	114
Belfast and Loose	119
Long Weekend	127
The Babysitter	135
Honey Wild and Manna-Dew	143
The Proudest Boast	155
Love Story (You and Me)	161
Son of Obituary	172
Bath Night	181
These Walls, Thy Sphere	187

FINE

CAFÉS OF DESIRE

"Is anyone sitting there?"

There was nobody sitting there. I confirmed this with haste that was just the right side of seemly. My body language changed. I pushed back into my seat and parted my legs. I was a chair asking her to sit on me. She didn't.

She quickly monopolised the table. I had a cup and saucer, spoon, an uneaten Italian biscuit, a notebook, a pen and a well-thumbed copy of Italo Calvino's *Mr Palomar*. These things were as nothing before the icebreaker of her handbag: the cup in its saucer chattered like teeth and the dog-eared book edged over the precipice. Her bag was large and black with pale cracks in the leather at each corner, fine as spiderwebs. There was something embossed on the side of the bag, or something had been pressed into its flesh. If it had once been legible, it was no longer the case: it was a scar now, pitted, semi-circular and with the gloss of skin mended over bone. The bag continued its voyage over the table, a black ship in full sail.

"Sorry," she said, diving into it and retrieving a pair of glasses which she put on. The lenses were scratched and smudged with fingerprints, and I could hardly see her eyes through the scuffed refraction of the café's strip-lighting. She whisked the bag off the table and onto her chair, rolling the coat from her shoulders and draping it over the chair-back. As she moved towards the counter, she half turned toward me: "Sorry. You don't mind, do you? The bag?"

"Of course," I said, meaning "Of course not." I looked at her, quite casually. She was slim and tall, with dark curling hair. She leaned into the curving counter as she talked to the barista, her hips resting on the swell of the glass display case. Her nose, with the glasses resting on it, was long and sharp. I returned to my notebook, but my thoughts were distracted, my gaze inevitably drawn back to her lively discussion over the artisan sausage rolls.

I looked at what I'd written. I'd come to this café to steal. I was writing a novel about an isolated man and was here for verisimilitude: the conversations of old ladies and young mums, that sort of thing. Life experiences our hero would never know; happy people knitted into the community in easily defined roles: the salt of the earth next to my stultifying clod. It wasn't working. Cafés were not the melting pots they used to be. At least this one wasn't. It was too upmarket, there was no grist. All human life was elsewhere—this was a middle-class verisimilitude I could fake in my sleep.

This part of town used to be dark with post-industrial grime, damp and clay grey, smelling of petrol and beer-farts and lining your nostrils with black grit. Now it looked like every other part of town, any town. The coffee had improved.

I looked toward the counter and the girl appeared to be in the middle of an animated conversation with the server. It wasn't aggressive, it was familiar, an ongoing conversation between old friends. I picked up the copy of *Mr Palomar* and looked again at my own inadequate notes. Calvino's prose was crisp and precise. The sentences were seamlessly dovetailed, even in translation. His writing was like a game of Jenga, sentences piled on top of one another, the process agonisingly teased out: the deliberate, detailed precision masking the writer's swagger, his poise. This was Calvino at the height of his powers, exulting in his own strength.

And I had written this sentence: "Robinson pushed his hand into the belly of the sofa and met something warm and solid, something hairy and lively with jagged little teeth." I striped the page with a fat, black line and looked over to see the girl but there was no sign of her. I looked at the bag. It was still there, the coat too. *Must have gone to the loo*, I thought.

I returned to the page, staring blankly at Robinson. I had no idea what to do with Robinson. I had forgotten who Robinson was. Why would my readers give a shit about Robinson if I knew nothing about him? What sort of a name was Robinson anyway? No one was called Robinson: it was a barley water, a racist jam, a desert island dweller with a stirring theme tune. It was an ersatz name: no one was *actually* called Robinson. People just assumed they were because it kept cropping up on *Neighbours*.

I ran a line through Robinson. It was a stupid, boring name and it was ruining my novel. How could someone called Robinson kill a vampire? Oh, yeah, there were vampires in it too. A Robinson could never dispatch a bloodsucker. You need a "van" something: Helsing? Hellsing? Killsing? Gogh? Dyke? Dyke-Parks? The Man?

Forget the van. It's been done to death.

How about Kincaid? Or Kindale? Carden? Clunes? Could a Clunes ever be a satisfactory protagonist in anything? Wishart? Bellamy? Benfield? Newman, Neumann, Garett, Parrott, Peters, Lee, Bassett, Bowley, Moncrieff, Hart, Atkins, Watkins, Pipkins. Smurfett, Parfitt, Rossi, Ball? Svenonius? Suzuki? Svenonius-Suzuki? Potter, Thatcher, Smith, Wainwright?

I was tentatively scratching in the name "Wainwright", when I noticed movement at the opposite side of the table. The girl was back.

"Thanks for looking after my bag," she said. "No problem," I said, looking up.

It was not the girl. It was certainly *a* girl, but it was not *the* girl, not the same girl.

"Sorry I was so long." she said. "No problem," I said, staring at her. She looked similar. Same build, same style of clothing. The hair was close. But they were not the same. If you'd seen her in passing you might have mistaken her for the same girl, but not me. I'd looked properly, I'd taken my time, and this was a completely different person. She reached for the handbag.

"What do you think you're doing?" I said.

"What do you mean?"

"I'm watching that bag for someone."

"Yes. But I'm back," she said.

"Nice try," I said, coolly.

"It's my bag. You saw me put it here."

"No. I saw someone put that bag there and when she returns, I'll gladly give it to her."

"It was me."

"C'mon!" There was an implied "love" at the end of the "c'mon", but I didn't say it in case it sounded sexist and patronising, even though I was in the right. "You haven't even made an effort: you're not dressed the same, your hair's wrong and, I hate to say it, but you're not as pretty. Sorry."

"I'm taking my fucking bag."

"No, you're not."

"Is there a problem?" said a passing barista, who may have been under the impression he was a policeman.

"I'm sorry?" I said, failing to recognise his authority, at least until he put the mop down. He directed the same question specifically to the girl.

"Is there a problem?"

"I asked this idiot to watch my bag and now he's saying it isn't mine."

"Well, it isn't."

"Oh, for fuck's sake!"

She swept up the bag and coat in a single movement and pushed into the street outside. I scrabbled to my feet, but the server blocked me.

"What are you doing? She's getting away."

"Leave it, *sir*," said the youth. The *sir* was a slight.

"You're abetting a crime," I said. We did a little dance, him jogging to one side in anticipation of me moving in that direction, and then moving in the other direction just as I had chosen to go that way. He'd have been a boon to any five-a-side team.

I scooped up my possessions, slipping the notebook, paperback and pens into the pockets of my raincoat.

"I have to go," I said. "I do *not* want to be here when the owner gets back." I punched my arms through the sleeves of my coat and limped toward the door as, in all the excitement, I hadn't noticed my foot had gone to sleep.

"I had a duty of care," I announced to the freshly interested café audience. They may have been middle-class, but they had the prurient appetite for spectacle of a nation raised on Jeremy Kyle. They were hoping for violence. I was hoping to cheat them of it, though I would have welcomed the lie-detector test.

I went outside. The street was oblivious: men in baseball caps trundled over the uneven paving on mobility scooters. Pigeons stabbed at discarded chip packets. On the other side of the street a youth with an arm in plaster noisily failed to make another jump on a skateboard. There was no sign of the girl in the stolen coat with the stolen bag. I tried for a moment to put myself in her shoes, to try and imagine where a girl who had just successfully committed daylight robbery would go next. But almost as quickly as I started, I gave up. Because how could I possibly know?

The Sound of Young People

I'M ON A BUS. I'm always on a bus. My car sits outside the flat, corroded with neglect like its owner. I never use it. It belongs to some other part of my life, a faded thing from a forgotten version of me, like my good silver or my penis. If I want to travel to and from work, I get a bus.

Buses used to be belching, bone-rattling things. They had poorly stuffed seats and weeping windows. I'm old enough to remember people smoking on buses. I'm *just* old enough to remember bus conductors: skinny, on-the-ration men with long, yellow teeth and lank hair falling over shiny, skin-dusted shoulders. I remember the smell. They smelled of the past: body odour, boiled cabbage, brilliantine and cigarette smoke, especially cigarette smoke. The smell of fags pressed itself into everything in the past: pub ceilings, piano keys, hospital waiting rooms, Lionel Jeffries' moustache. The smell of cigarettes is the smell of the 20th Century and, as cancerous and problematic as that century was, it seems as hard to give up.

Buses were a place of comfort when I was a kid, like being in a lively front room or a Saturday morning cinema. Anybody might turn up, all colours, all ages, all sitting and shouting and smoking. The driver's forearm hung from the cab window as he barked out place names, lips clamped around a tight Woodbine. The conductor's sea-legs nimbly negotiated the corridor like a strutting greaser working a waltzer, his ticket machine lively on his hip, a gun-slinger's holster.

Buses are not like that now. They are long and silent and vacuum packed. The driver is a distant figure operating under glass, remote as God. You pay with your phone before you even get on. Everything is grey or purple: sober, important colours, and the seats are high, set on plinths to discourage the elderly, the young, the differently abled, all the natural customers of a bus service. Even the vulcanised nooses meant for strap-hanging are intimidatingly high: you must be this tall to ride. The destinations are pre-recorded and rolled out in a bright and slightly disengaged manner, suggesting the placenames had been recorded in bits and assembled like linguistic Meccano, or the speaker had never been human and was one of those home-help A.I.s developed to sound warm and interested, while failing to recognise your favourite album and covertly recording all your conversations.

I vibrated gently on my plinth. Through the dark glass I could see traffic in the road about me, low and close. Anally fixated Audi drivers sniffed the bumper of the car in front. I felt like Zeus on Olympus, or Jean-Luc Picard on the bridge of the Enterprise.

I'd missed the rush-hour by staying late at the office. Intending to do some work, I was distracted reading about "The Mad Gasser of Mattoon", which led me down a rabbit hole of Moth and Owl men, and whole subspecies of American mythological oddities. By the time I'd run out of cryptozoological nonsense, it was 8.30, I'd done no work, and decided to go home.

It was a dark night, and the inside of the bus was projected onto the black windows, the muted neon of passing shops and headlamps became phosphorescent ghosts drifting between the tight squares of yellow and white light gridding the glass.

What a rubbish day.

A meeting with another department saw me stumble over some figures, and a recent pointless and expensive tech upgrade meant I was no longer able to do my basic job requirements and, being a man, I hadn't asked anyone for help. Instead, I sat in my office with my head in my hands reading about "The Mad Gasser of Mattoon". I resolved to get someone from I.T. to tell me how my computer worked in the morning. I could live with the rolled eyes and heavy sighs. I was used to them.

Tonight, I would relax with a glass of wine and some vinyl. I'd wear headphones so I wouldn't disturb the woman upstairs, not that she ever complained. I wonder what she's like. I'd met her once, but I was quite drunk and could only remember the sketchiest details: dark hair, thin, big nose. We hadn't become fast friends, which was probably my fault. I'd likely said or done something. Historically, that's often been the case. Whatever happened, she hasn't been round for so much as a cup of tea or to complain about the smell. I do occasionally hear her stomping about, playing music. I think she works from home as she doesn't seem to leave the flat often, except when she clanks back from the off-licence. I hear that.

Staring out the bus window, I was suddenly aware of noise: invasive, high and angry, like a hornet trapped in a tin can. It was followed by a supplementary disturbance: louder, more exuberant, territorial. It was the sound of young people. Young people were announcing their presence, their agency; young people were pushing against boundaries. They got on the bus behind me, phones blaring. It sounded like they were listening to an underground station, the music all repetitive beats and shout-outs, but it was difficult to hear with the boys screaming over one another. There were four of them, I think—I didn't look round. They were probably black, but who knew? All young people sounded the same now.

They were mucking about, a time-honoured tradition at the back of the bus. I think even I might have done it when I was younger, albeit quietly. They're just kids, I thought, kids trying to have a bit of fun, kids trying to get on in a society that wants to tell them off, to put them in a box before they've even discovered who they are. They're unchaperoned on a bus at nine o' clock at night: of course, they're going to act up. Good for them.

There's so much pressure on young people now: all those exams, a future without stability, never being able to afford a house, never being able to pay off their student loans. Social media influencers, cyber bullies, stabbings, aggressive performative pornography, and people my age telling them that their music is rubbish—it is, but that's not their fault. That's a *crushing* amount of pressure. No wonder they play up. No wonder they kick back. I can't blame them.

Still.

Stabbings.

There have always been stabbings. Stabbings aren't new. Stabbings are a constant in society, in all societies, except, perhaps, in America where you can get a gun if you collect three Slim Jim wrappers. Knives are cheaper, more readily available, and quieter than guns. They're also more personal. You really need to get *in* there with a knife. You get to look them in the eye while they're bleeding out. You get to see them *know* they're dying. It's intimate. It's more violent than a gun. Nastier.

I give the boys a quick look. Three of them are white. They're in school uniform. The black one, though—he's six feet. He slouches at the back, face half hidden by a baseball cap and hoodie. He's the one playing the music. The other three are a foot shorter than him. They're the ones fooling about, practically children. They're swearing and calling each other queer for the thrill of acting up. But he isn't—he's all but ignoring them, focused on the tinny beats from his phone, head bobbing.

I look forward again and I check my phone. An e-mail from Tim at work about a Peter Strickland film he's desperate to see. I'm not going to the cinema with another middle-aged man, Tim, for fuck's sake.

The noise abated as, one by one, and in a volley of unimaginative insults, the boys departed the bus. The music continued however: the thud, the crackle, the buzz. The bus made an abrupt jolt on a corner and, behind me, something metallic dropped onto the floor.

Shit.

The music continued and I sat it out, only daring to look round once the shockwave had died down. The black boy was still there, bent over his phone, face missing. We were alone on the bus by now.

It didn't *have* to be a knife, of course. It could have been any metal object falling from his person onto the floor: a silver cigarette case or a fob watch or a large, loose signet ring. It didn't have to be a knife.

The music was cutting out now, stuttering. He filled the gaps with low, spat invective. He was suddenly very angry at something, and I was the only thing near enough to be angry at.

I pulled my phone from my pocket and started swiping through pages, my thumb oozing like the belly of a gastropod, trailing across the screen. No messages: a friend request from a girl in a bikini from Belize. She had thirty-four friends but none of them were from Belize. I didn't confirm.

The music choked into silence. The bell on the bus rang and a stop-sign flashed red. I kept my head down as I heard footsteps behind me. They stopped short.

"Hey mate."

He sounded like a man. How old was this kid? How many years had he been kept back in class? Was this the cause of his anger and disillusionment? That he was twenty-five and still learning trigonometry? I ignored him, blinkering my vision until the universe was a flat, square screen resting in the palm of my hand. I had finally caught up with the rest of the world, and all it had taken was the threat of violent assault on public transport.

"Mate."

Hard. Impatient. Borderline aggressive. What had I ever done to him? Except ignore him the first time. Did I look like one of his teachers? Did I look like a teacher who had put him down and made him feel worthless? Was the teacher racist? Did I look like his racist teacher? I wasn't racist, I didn't think. I'm sure there were loads of non-racist things I'd done in the past, none of which I could recall at that exact moment. I saw the Bhundu Boys in concert in Finsbury Park. I wore a "Rock against Racism" badge. I boycotted South Africa in the eighties. It was a low-level boycotting—I didn't have much business with South Africa—but in principle I wanted nothing to do with it. I certainly ate fewer grapes. If I'd been in Queen I'd have attempted to veto the Sun City gig. I'd have to abide by the majority vote—Queen was a democracy, that was just one of the ironies of Queen, but . . .

"For fuck's sake . . ."

I remembered that I still had the "Rock against Racism" badge on the lapel of my jacket. I found myself pushing it out with my thumb, so he would see it before he saw my face. I turned to look up at him.

He looked about thirteen. He was tall but he had the face of a child. His skin hairless and taut and while he was frowning right now, I knew the moment he stopped the wrinkle would smooth away to pacific calm.

"Can I help you?" I said, trying not to sound smug and white. He'd probably been talked down to by middle-aged white men his whole life. All thirteen years of it.

"Your wallet," he said.

Ah. I was being mugged after all. There were cameras on this bus. He'd never get away with it. But the cameras were above him and he was wearing a baseball cap, his face invisible. He *would* get away with it. Balls. Well, I wasn't going to make it easy for him. Equally I wasn't going to make it so hard for him he murdered me.

I was going to have to find a third way: a way to both live and to live with myself.

"I'm afraid I'm not going to give you my wallet," I said. Something flickered in his face, a note of confusion relaxing into a sort of angry acceptance. He pushed something at me, and I flinched. It was my wallet.

"It was on the floor," he said, "fell out when you took your phone out of your pocket."

I went to take it from his hand, but he dropped it in my lap.

"Thank you so much," I said as he turned away. The bus had reached his stop. In his hand was his phone, the screen cracked, white filigree spread from one corner, fine as lace.

"Really. Thank you so much."

As the doors opened, he turned and loudly sucked his teeth at me before stepping off the bus, as he knew I was expecting him to do.

Fine.

And This Is Me...

- I'm Paul Reverb. I'm a man in my mid-fifties.
- I have a Belgian grandmother. That's the most exotic thing about me.
- I no longer have a Belgian grandmother. Apart from an aunt and three cousins, two of whom I've never met, I have no family.
- I own my own flat. It used to belong to my parents, and I moved out for twenty years, but when they died, I moved back in again. That was ten years ago.
- I have most of my own teeth, though my gums are set at a permanent low tide.
- I've never had a major operation or stayed overnight in hospital. There are two scars on my body. The one under my eyebrow is from chicken pox. The other, on my top lip, is from a needlessly aggressive mugging. The mugger got away with my Walkman, a cassette of Kate Bush's *The Whole Story* (slightly defective: there was an early fade on the "Wuthering Heights" guitar coda) and a bacon and cream cheese bagel. He snapped my front tooth, split my lip and broke my nose with one punch. This took place on my doorstep, my key already in the lock. He tapped me on the shoulder and punched me unconscious. I woke up bleeding, the contents of my bag strewn over the pavement. They never got him. Hard to fence a bagel.

- I own two thousand vinyl records. I have a thousand DVDs and five hundred CDs, and I still have a VHS collection. My living room is a landfill of dead media.
- I work in an office. That's all I wish to say about that.
- I was born on the day that *Sgt. Pepper's Lonely Hearts Club Band* was released. That makes me a Gemini if you're wondering. I used to think this was a fun, quirky fact to bring up at parties and on first dates. At this point I don't mention it at all. Too aging. It's history now, barely even Common Era.
- I think I'm named for Beatle Paul, though while my parents lived through the sixties, they were not of it. Could have been worse. I think Ringo Reverb would have made for a difficult childhood.
- I have large, flat feet with narrow heels. I go through a lot of blister plasters when I buy new shoes.
- I've never been married. Not even close, really.
- I'm a heterosexual man.
- I've slept with nineteen women in my life. Apparently, that's quite a bit above average, but stretched out over fifty odd years it doesn't seem like a lot. Most of them were in my early twenties, and it's fallen off a bit lately. I've been averaging a fuck a decade for the last decade.
- I've had two serious relationships. One lasted two years, the other lasted three years. I believed I was deeply in love on both occasions. No, I *was* deeply in love. It wasn't my choice to end either relationship.
- My favourite thing to cook for myself is steak. I like it medium rare. I cook each side for ten seconds, flip it, then cook the other side for ten seconds before flipping it back again, on a griddle pan to keep it moist. I'm not sure where I picked up this technique. At around the halfway mark, I paint mustard on each side of the steak and add salt and pepper. When it's cooked, I let it rest, oozing blood onto the plate, and melt Roquefort cheese over it. I buy a big steak, so I don't tend to have anything with it, just steak and cheese. It's delicious.

It does tend to rather glaze the hob, and the kitchen stinks of fat for a couple of days afterwards. But it's worth it. It's not really a health tool.
- I was briefly a vegetarian in my teens, mainly to impress a girl who went hunt saboteuring. It didn't work out. Well, it worked out for the fox, so that's something.
- I like old films, black and white British ones, filmed before I was born. As I get older, I find I have nostalgia for a place I've never known, a non-existent English Arcadia. This is the fatal weakness of the British people: we're doomed to long for our imaginary Empire.
- I've taken out over-fifties' life insurance. Someone will be obliged to bury me when I die. It's paid for.
- I was never a mod growing up, but I find I've started to dress like someone who used to be a mod. Even my hair looks sort of modish. I don't think I ever deliberately made that choice. It just happened.
- I'm not scared of dying. But I'm scared of being ill and alone.
- That said I'm not looking for a nursemaid. I think I'm good for a few years yet. If I ever had another relationship, she would not be expected to wipe my arse. Though it would be a bonus as I went into my decline.
- When my doctor asks me how many units of alcohol I consume in a week, I divide the amount by ten. And then she tells me I'm drinking too much.
- I'm quite tall.
- My back hurts all the time. I've had bad posture for half a century, five decades of stooping so people can talk to me without feeling intimidated. Forty years of standing at the front of gigs so no one else can see.
- (I never do that. I stand at the bar and nod gently, regardless of the band. I haven't touched a crash barrier since 1985).

- The Smiths are my favourite band. I've always been slightly embarrassed by this, and these days it's almost an admission personal wrong-doing. But it's true.
- My favourite book is *Leave it to Psmith* by P.G. Wodehouse. Wodehouse is, I think, the funniest writer of all time, though I wonder if he's rather lost-in-translation for modern readers. I mean, I didn't grow up in the 1920s and I've never had a valet or belonged to a Gentlemen's club, but I grew up *reading* about that stuff. It was in comics. I don't suppose people do anymore. I wonder if P.G. Wodehouse is still funny if you grew up with Jeremy Clarkson books in the house.
- I have two middle names: Eduard and Antoine. I was named for my Belgian Grandmother's uncle apparently. I don't know why. I've never been to Belgium, and I think most of that side of my family were killed in the First World War, and comprehensively wiped out in the Second. I should really do some Ancestry.com stuff and find out if I'm related to Jacques Brel or Hergé. Let's hope it's not Hergé, I think he was a Nazi.
- I've looked it up: the worst you could say about Hergé was he was a collaborator, which is still pretty bad. He was very right wing but probably not as right wing as my dad.
- You might have noticed my initials spell the word P.E.A.R. It wasn't lost on the boys at my comprehensive, who called me "Hairy Pear", as I was the first boy in class to hit puberty. This was later shortened to H.P. when it was also discovered my parents were paying for our television in instalments. I'm happy to say I no longer know anyone from school.
- My first memory of school is of a girl called Jane Moran crying while sitting on a rocking horse. There was a rocking horse in my primary school. I sound Victorian. We also had chalk slates, rickets and the birch.
- We didn't have the birch. We *did* have the cane, though. I was never caned. I wasn't the type. I sat in the middle-rows and kept my head

down. Rougher, louder boys, boys whose families wanted them out of school and working were the ones who got caned. Boys who never had the proper blazer or rugby shirt, boys who were beaten for being poor.

— I got detention once, when I dropped a folded-up page from a copy of *Mayfair* in science class and Gary Lloyd found it and told the teacher. I got a stern talking to and she threatened to tell my parents, until I started crying and she relented. She made me write an essay on "self-pollution". Perhaps I did go to school in the Victorian era.

— I can still vividly remember the girl in the picture. It was given to me by Anthony Hammill in exchange for issue eight of *2000AD* comic (it featured "eight full colour monster pix!" but the real draw was the unmasking of *Judge Dredd* for the first and, as far as I know, only time). Anthony had found a full magazine in the park which was incredibly rare. Bush-porn was normally torn up and scattered over railway cuttings, a manifestation of the inner turmoil of the remorseful masturbator. Anthony's *Mayfair* had been carefully asset stripped and he'd made a killing. He had an almost complete set of *Star Wars* cards by this time, wrapped in thick rubber bands and bulging impressively in his trouser pocket. He asked a high price for his pornography but, as he pointed out, it wasn't just the picture—there was an article on sand dune racing in Tunisia on the back, and so it was educational too.

The girl was a beautiful glossy brunette in a bathroom that didn't look like our bathroom. No one would have placed a Spanish dancer over the toilet brush holder in this bathroom. She stood, braced in the doorway, her arms raised and her red lips slightly parted, and wore nothing but a fur coat and high heels. The heels matched the lipstick. I couldn't believe the indecency of it: she was wearing outerwear but no underwear. How was this possible? It smashed through all known social laws. Whole new worlds of erotic

possibility opened to me: she wasn't wearing pants and she didn't mind who knew.
— Losing that picture to the teacher was a formative experience. I'd never known true unhappiness until that point.
— I don't remember much about my childhood. Vague memories of seeing the sea and a bigger boy throwing a plastic bag full of snails at my head in Easthill Park. I remember being four and crying because I couldn't tie my shoelaces, but I needed to learn before starting school. I remember the feeling of not wanting to go to school. I still have that feeling.
— My favourite aftershave is *Eucris* by Geo. F. Trumper. It's a musky, manly smell and comes in a cool, Victorian style medicine bottle. James Bond uses *Eucris* hair tonic in Ian Fleming's books and I tried that too, but it doesn't really do anything. Smells nice, though.
— My first love was Felicity Kendall. That's not quite true: my first love was Barbara Good played by Felicity Kendall in *The Good Life*. If you watch it again Barbara is still spirited, funny, practical, nurturing and sexy. Whereas Tom, her husband, is just a selfish prick. I still love Barbara Good.
— My second crush was Jodie Foster in *Candleshoe*. And then Judi Bowker in *Clash of the Titans*. All blondes. In about 1981 I saw a picture of Kate Bush and switched teams forever. Sorry blondes.
— I've been single for nine years.
— I've been an orphan for ten. My last relationship would probably have ended a lot sooner if my parents hadn't died (car crash). I don't think she wanted to leave me while I was grieving. So, she gave it another year. It was kind of her. A twelve-month pity fuck.
— My favourite records are *Starsailor* by Tim Buckley, *Mark Hollis* by Mark Hollis, *69* by A R Kane, *The Something Rain* by Tindersticks, *Southpaw Grammar* by Morrissey, *Explosions in the Glass Palace* by The Rain Parade, *Rock Bottom* by Robert Wyatt, *Delay 1968* by Can, *Meat is Murder* by The Smiths and *Toxic* by Britney Spears. People think

I'm being a smart-arse when I say I like *Toxic*, but I really do. It's brilliant.

— I'm writing a book, a novel. I've been trying to write a novel, or at least talking about writing a novel, for twenty years. And I really do want to write a novel; I'm not sure I want to write the novel I'm writing.
— It's not that I'm lazy (it is partly that I'm lazy). I've written a lot of the book and I think some of it is quite good. I'm just not sure that my ideas are very good. Or commercial. Or make sense. I wish I had someone to ask. Someone I loved or trusted or both. Someone to talk to.
— Before this I wanted to be a pop star. That didn't happen either.
— I just don't want to be someone who works in an office. I want to live.

The Pint of No Return

I was drinking with my two oldest friends: Scott and Brendan. Scott I'd known twenty years, and he was the most enthusiastic man I'd ever met, in that he had many, many interests. Brendan, I'd known even longer. He was whatever the opposite of an enthusiast was. Brendan liked only two things: The Beatles and particle physics. Everything else was beneath his consideration and existed only to be sneered at. He was a barren planet on an erratic orbit between twin stars, a celestial ping-pong ball.

Brendan and I may have had something in common when we were younger, but I couldn't remember what it was. We were now friends only because we'd always been friends. I wasn't sure we liked each other, but we were friends so liking one another was a minor detail.

Brendan sat bent over the pub table, scowling at his pint, occasionally flipping a beer mat in the air and catching it with the tenacity of a dog that had developed opposable thumbs. I could feel the vibration of his feet tapping under the table. He had a lot of nervous energy, his body permanently vibrating. Brendan had once been beautiful, with dark hair, pale skin and large, blue eyes framed by long lashes. His mother had doted on him as a child and, as an adult, women and men had exhaled involuntarily in his wake. Eyelashes had been batted at him so furiously and for so long he had a permanent quiff. But a short-lived, ill-advised marriage had done nothing for his temper, and a penchant for drinking and fighting had coarsened and swollen his face, ravaged his teeth and obliterated his address book. The long lashes were now hidden behind heavily framed glasses and his hair was greying and unwashed. A mustard-coloured stripe stained his widow's peak, the result of many decades smoking. His teeth were like gravel. None of these vicissitudes had dampened his self-regard. He still saw himself a lady's man, which he never had been, and was confounded and hurt when his attentions were rebuffed. This would lead to long nights of poisonous trolling on the internet, until he passed out, glass in hand.

Scott had none of Brendan's natural advantages: he'd been a skinny boy, with lank blonde hair, a large red nose that seemed permanently wet at the nostril. His teeth soft and yellow as buttermilk. He'd been severely bullied as a child and consequently stayed in his house, reading comics and playing games on his computer. It stood him in good stead as he now owned his own computer business and was doing very nicely. He had also, miraculously, grown into his looks and, perhaps more miraculously, retained his hair. His teeth were now very straight, very white, and very new. He never drank beer, favouring gin and slimline. He wore a coat that cost a month's rent and talked about the Japanese TV series *The Water Margin*, which he'd been watching again. He'd enjoyed it, but as Brendan pointed out, Scott enjoyed everything. Scott smiled, and it was like someone opened a fridge door.

I began to think about friendship: male friendship, which is the worst kind of friendship. What are friends for? Why do we have them? What function do they serve? I sat there with these two men as they squabbled and blustered, and my eyes drifted around the room. I'd have preferred to have been at any other table. Over there two beautiful student girls were chatting. One of them was wearing dungarees and a cardigan. She wore badges and I wondered what they said. That could be a conversation starter. There was a chap in big round specs tapping at a laptop. He might have been trying to write a book like me. We could swap tips. Maybe *he'd* have liked the idea of a vampire hypnotist. No, I'd probably have to build up to mentioning that. Develop some trust between us first. You couldn't go in cold with a vampire hypnotist. I looked at the server. When I was in this pokey little bar, with these two friends, I looked at the server a lot. Brendan and Scott would've called her a barmaid, but I knew that the preferred nomenclature nowadays is *server*.

"Yeah, you like that, don't you?" said Brendan.

"I like what?"

"You like her being a server, don't you? It's one etymological mince away from being a servant. You'd love that. Your lot do."

Oh yes, I forgot. There were elements of class war enshrined in my relationship with Brendan. His parents were Irish immigrants and his enormous family had moved down from Manchester when Brendan was twelve, so he was both foreign and Northern, an unassailable argument winner in the eighties. They settled in a slightly rougher part of our hometown. Given the town we were from, I suggested this was like one pig telling another pig that there was a better quality of shit in his part of the sty, but Brendan advised me I'd betrayed myself in calling the working classes pigs. I pointed out that I had nothing growing up, whereas he had all the latest games and action figures and bikes. Yeah, the working-classes don't know how to budget do they, Paul? They spend all their money on gadgets and gewgaws because they like bright shiny things and don't know any better. I bet you hate walking past an estate and seeing all those big plasma screens nailed to the walls, blaring out *X Factor* and quality period drama on ITV. And at this point he'd won the argument, as he knew that I *do* hate those big tellies people attach to their walls. Then he sloped off to the toilet for a victory piss and I was left to consider my privilege once again.

"What's wrong with 'barmaid', Verbo?" said Scott, who had been paying closer attention to his phone than the court proceedings unfolding in front of him.

"They just prefer server," I said.

"Who?"

"Barmaids."

"Fair enough. If that's what they're happy with then I'll go along with that."

"Right, yeah? Fair enough. No problem."

"It's because 'maid' implies virginity. And obviously no barmaids are virgins."

Brendan had returned from the toilets. He was still doing up his flies as he walked through the bar. A droplet of piss bloomed at his crotch. As he sat, he emitted a short, high-pitched fart like a steam whistle, and the shadow of panic passed over his face. He recovered quickly, a cat after a fall.

Brendan was five pints in. This was the danger point: the pint of no return. After another drink Scott would be making his excuses, and I would be left to listen to Brendan's rambling and bitter tirade against women, and then tasked with escorting the stumbling ingrate home. He never said thank you. More than anything, that was what annoyed me: the contrarian arguments, the endless trolling on social media, the calling of taxis and ambulances, the apologies to taxi and ambulance drivers, all the long tedious evenings listening to him slur his way through a Christmas list of my shortcomings in an increasingly impenetrable Northern accent. All of that would have been fine if he'd just apologised. If he'd taken me to one side and said "Mate, I know I'm a bit of a handful and I just wanted you to know I appreciate all the things you've done for me." And then we'd have an awkward, no-cocks-touching hug and never talk about it again.

It never happened. He didn't even remember half of it, and the bits he did remember he imagined he was a lovable rogue, and I was just expected to put up with this behaviour because we were always, immutably, friends forever and ever. And I did put up with it because I had no other friends. The philosopher Sting once said: if you love somebody set them free. I was fairly certain I didn't *love* Brendan; my affection had long ago curdled into something more like acceptance or exhaustion. Experts tell you that you need to let go of toxic people to learn to love yourself, but that was where Brendan had me over a barrel—he knew deep down I hated myself far more than I hated him.

Scott had no trouble with any of this. He was a blithe, frictionless man, never quite in the moment, his attention always somewhere else. I imagined he played a mean game of chess. He bought a last round of drinks and somehow managed to get table service from the server. She came over with the tray and Scott paid her with a large denomination note and advised her to keep the change without looking up from his phone. That's how you get table service. Brendan unashamedly stared at the server's cleavage throughout the transaction, but at least he didn't say anything. I over-smiled and over-thanked and made far too much eye-contact. I couldn't help it. In my feeble, middle-aged, and lonely way I was in love with her. Scott didn't notice—he'd already called a taxi using an app on his phone. It was mildly disconcerting going for a drink with someone who never took their coat off, but he was pleasant enough company when he engaged with his environment. In a sense we were both living virtual lives, but at least his was well paid.

Brendan, of course, noticed my over-attentive display. Like all true misogynists, he had extraordinary antennae for finer feelings in the breast of his fellow man, and a commensurate level of scorn.

"Chuck E's in love!" he said.

"What's this?" said Scott, "who's in love?"

"Brendan's being hilarious again."

"At least I can be when I want to be," said Brendan, "when it's required. Our boy here has got a thing for the 'server'. Look at him: all dry teeth and wet palms. Go and ask her out. She's an Art History student. Maybe she could do some restoration work."

She *was* an Art History student, though I wasn't sure how Brendan knew this. Her name was Kat. She was 22 and she was thin with big eyes and big hair. She had gaps between her teeth and dressed like a bandit queen in a low budget science fiction film. My infatuation brimmed over like boiling milk whenever she came near me. It had spilled in front of Brendan now and was hissing up at him from the table.

Sometimes I'd come into the bar early intending to do some writing, and it would be just Kat and me. We'd say hello and I'd find a seat and pretend to write while she went about the place with a cloth cleaning the tables. And when she got to my table, she'd ask me how the book was going and I'd tell her and she would look genuinely interested, and she would joke that I could sign a copy for her when I was famous, and I'd say you'll be famous long before me and we'd both agree that that was probably correct. Then she'd go back behind the bar, and I would do some work instead of pretending to. On one occasion I recklessly sat at the bar, and we had quite a long chat about art until her boyfriend came in. He was six-foot four and in a band. Handsome, if you like that sort of thing, and she clearly did. Who's in a band nowadays? Who wants bands? Why couldn't he do something useful like pull plastic out of the sea or give mouth to mouth to a dying bee? The planet's on its arse, mate, and you're fucking about in a band? I don't mind—I'll be dead by the time it all goes properly to shit, but you and your children will be sailing the swollen seas in a coracle made of human skin and drinking each other's wee, and not for pleasure either, though he looks the type. He's in a band: I'm sure his achingly tender love songs will be of tremendous comfort when she's sold to the highest bidder by a pirate with a necklace of human ears.

"Guys, I'm gonna chip," said Scott, rising and slipping his phone into his pocket in one smooth gesture, as though he were practising Tai Chi. A taxi beeped for him in the street outside and he gave a practiced wave.

"Where do you think you're going?" said Brendan, "Have another one. Don't be a prick."

"Sorry lads," said Scott, not even considering it.

"Go on. Paul's going to ask the barmaid . . . server, out."

"Really?" said Scott.

"Obviously not."

Scott popped his collar and left without looking back. The opening and shutting of the door sent a sudden arctic blast into the bar.

"He's a wanker," said Brendan, draining his glass. "Couple more?"

His face had taken on an oily glow. Beer suds collected at the corners of his mouth like alluvial silt. His eyes were small, glassy, and staring at a fixed point which was five inches to the left of my head. I made a quick calculation: things were about to get louder and fightier. If I refused him a pint there would be consequences. If he went to the bar there would be consequences. If I attempted to leave there would be consequences. I chose the lesser of three evils.

"I'll get these, Brendy."

"You are a gentleman," he said, "you posh prick." I went to the bar.

"Is he alright?" said Kat, before taking my order.

"Yeah, he's fine."

"Only, he's not normally alright. Normally he's a bloody nuisance. I've had to chuck him out of here before now."

She was perturbed. She bit her lip. I saw a flash of uneven white teeth. She looked like Whistler's "Portrait of Lady Meux", but with fewer clothes on. This was the only place in the world that I wanted to be.

"He's fine," I said, "He's just had a few."

She looked at me doubtfully. "So, you're buying him another one, are you?"

I smiled, she tutted and poured two more pints.

"How do you know him anyway?" she said, taking my money. "You seem like quite different people." This was the closest thing I'd had to a compliment in about three years, and it was from Kat. I beamed.

"He's just a mate. Known him years. Feel like I've always known him. Can't shake him off."

"Like a cold sore," she said.

"I haven't got herpes," I said, abruptly.

Her eyes widened. They really were big eyes.

"Glad to hear it."

"Complex *or* simplex."

I headed back to the table to die quietly. *I haven't got herpes*. Why not fish an AIDS test out of your wallet while you're at it? Brendan was leaning back in his chair, arms folded, eyes closed. The sound of glass hitting table nudged him into consciousness.

"You should you know," he said.

"What?"

"Ask her out."

"I just told her I didn't have herpes."

"Complex or simplex?"

"Both."

"Good start. Clean bill of health. That's what they like now. Ask her."

"I could be her dad."

"Doubtful," said Brendan, drawing steadily on his pint. "Now *I* could be her dad. Oh yes, I were quite the lady's man, back in the day. But you . . . unlikely. These days though . . . I mean you've got your own place. You're solvent. You wear colourful socks and that. Maybe she's into it . . ."

"She has a boyfriend."

"A lot of 'em do, a lot of 'em do. Doesn't mean nothing. I could tell you some stories . . ."

"You have, frequently. I'm going for a piss."

"I could tell you some stories," he shouted at my back. I didn't turn around.

The toilets were cold and small. There was condensation on the windows, and it dripped down the chipped green tiles making them clammy to the touch. The trough was a basic stainless-steel model that buckled and groaned with the temperature change as my steaming piss hit it. I relaxed and let out a fart. It's been happening a lot lately. I chased a piece of toilet cake towards the drain with my foaming effluent, the noise impressively redolent of sustained pressure. The prostate was good for a few years yet. There was no graffiti to read, which surprised me. Nowadays I cannot get through bodily functions: bathing, shitting, brushing my teeth, without reading something. It's boring to be tied to this tyranny of physicality: why can't we just *be*, instead of constantly having to push stuff into us and then squeeze it all out again, ruined. The giant sea cucumber eats with its anus. Why not? Cut out the middleman, that's what I say. So, I like to read when I'm going through the digestive rote. I can usually make it through a restaurant meal or a date without surreptitiously squinting at my phone, but not always.

As the power was draining from my flow, I heard a commotion. There was a loud crash, splintering glass and raised voices. Brendan. I tried to shake off the last of the piss, but it kept coming in useless little dribbles. The noise was getting worse. C'mon. Christ, what had he done now? I decided to risk it and returned my penis to my trousers. An immediate warm slick ran down my left thigh. I didn't get to wash my hands. Once again, my association with Brendan had led to a lowering of personal standards.

He was on the floor, leaning back on one hand with the other one raised over his head to fend off assault. In front of him stood Kat who was attempting to separate Brendan from the man with the glasses and the laptop. The laptop was on the floor and the man's table was on its side. Brendan's catalogue jeans were tiger striped with either spilled beer or urine. In the past he would have tried to fight the man, but the fight was gone from him. He looked frightened and confused. He flinched as I picked him up by the shoulders until he saw that it was me.

"Tell him, Paul. Explain. I was going to talk to the barmaid. Ask her out for you."

"What?" said Kat.

"He's drunk."

"Get him out of here."

"Of course."

"And don't you come back either."

"Right."

"What about my laptop?" said the speccy man. "And my beer?"

"Fucking hell," said Kat, "I can do you a beer, alright? I can't help with your computer. Okay?" He stood there. He had no idea what to do. He wasn't a habitual bar brawler.

I got Brendan back to my flat whereupon he produced a bottle of red wine from somewhere with the flourish of a stage magician. He was asleep on my sofa before he'd finished the first glass. I threw a blanket over him and poured a glass of wine for myself and sat in the semi-darkness listening to the rumble of the traffic outside. Three quarters of the way through the bottle it began to rain, a sudden heavy squall. I got up and looked at the empty, wet street outside.

"Thanks for looking after me, Paul," Brendan had said, seconds before losing consciousness.

"That's alright, mate." It was the first time he had ever thanked me for anything, and I was surprised at how much it moved me. Sudden stinging tears filled my eyes.

"I mean it," he said, starting to trail off. "You're my least embarrassing mate."

Summertime Special

I WAS ON HOLIDAY by myself. One of the few things I like about being single is going on holiday by myself. I was in a theatre bar called The Colonnade in Brighton and everything was red velvet and chintz. There were tainted mirrors and Spotlight photos of all the actors who had trod the boards of the adjoining theatre, luminaries such as Gabrielle Drake, Robert Gillespie and Michael Sharvell-Martin, whom I was particularly pleased to have spotted. He was the neighbour who drank home-brew in a shed with William Gaunt in the sit-com *No Place Like Home*. Gaunt was also there but you sort of expected him. He was a trouper.

Four immaculately groomed young men shimmered into the bar and immediately started talking about seeing Elton John's last tour and trying on each other's ponchos. This was Brighton then: the bar maid's hairdresser bred seahorses in his basement.

I was either on a sentimental journey or in the throes of a midlife crisis. I'd returned to Brighton the city where I was brought up. My hotel was in Regent's Square, one of those imposing white buildings that sidle up the Brighton coast like horse-shoe crabs: Georgian, shabby chic, picture-perfect with a crumbling glaze. There was a central reservation that had been converted, practically invisibly, into an underground car park and at the end of the road, staring out to sea, his fist aloft in defiance, was a big bronze sailor on a plinth, the embodiment of the British navies and, as it said on the plaque, "Our First Defence". They had built a wind-farm directly in front of him, which lent the statue an unintended quixotic quality.

The hotel had a small and beautifully turned-out breakfast room full of silent women eating on their own. If I were Alan Bennett or Muriel Spark, I could have probably got a novel out of it. It was unrealistically English—a pall of uptight silence fell over the room, challenged only by the grinding of recalcitrant organic muesli, chewed a joyless but sensible 36 times. One woman briefly complained about the "hardness" of her pineapple, but immediately apologised for complaining. The worst thing you could do here was make a fuss. You could hear a pin drop, though no one would be frivolous enough to drop a perfectly good pin.

Brighton was a palimpsest. I'd been here, approximately, every ten years since I left at the age of 13, and the only landmarks that remained were the Old Steine, the Pier and the Pavilion. Oh, and the sea. The sea was usually there. And unlike everything else in Brighton, the sea wasn't propped up by scaffolding, unless you counted the West Pier, a charcoal spider on the horizon that looked like Stromberg's sea-base after James Bond had a go at it. But I could never find specific things, half-remembered and long dead shops in The Lanes or the whereabouts of Uncle Sam's, the burger franchise that offered up The Blue Cheeseburger, and which was my first glimpse of artery-hardening heaven. There was no trace of it.

Portslade was where I grew up, though I've always said Brighton to avoid confusion. It felt exactly as it had done 35 years ago, and as soon as I reached Station Road, I had my bearings. The shops in the High Street had changed but the mood, the weather-beaten, overlooked atmosphere of the place, remained unchanged. I remembered there was an ice-cream shop staffed by a man in a crisp lab-coat, a dead-ringer for George Christie with his balding brilliantine head and the impenetrable whites of his granny glasses. I remembered a novelty shop that sold knock-off *Jim'll Fix It* badges. There's no sign of either, but they should still both be there. They fit the vibe. Portslade has not changed. I love it.

I thought back to that man, a man who wore a tie to work in an ice cream shop, a man with shiny round head and who smoked his woodbines wearing gloves so he wouldn't stain his fingers, and I think about how old I am now. My childhood took place in the distant past, in a narrow, alien world. It was a grim, grimy place, with pockets of desperate order, like this pristine man in his spotless shop. We used to laugh at people washing their doorsteps. It was a Canute-like attempt at control. The world outside was howling chaos, but not this little Englishman's castle. The portcullis was down and none shall pass. And take your bloody shoes off, while you're about it.

I laughed when I saw the alleyway snaking from the high street towards my primary school. I hadn't thought about it in decades. It was known locally as *The Twitten*, and I was amazed it was still there. The "Smile: You're on CCTV" posters were new, as was the razor wire and scaffolding that pressed in from the backside of the supermarket, but the snicket cut along exactly as it did in my childhood, delivering me 200 yards from my school, of which I could see virtually nothing as it was surrounded by giant walls that were not there in the seventies. It seemed a bit much. With everything we know now, it seems we were far more likely to be molested in the past, but maybe that was because we didn't have the big walls. The small roundabout outside the school and the block of flats opposite, "Vale Court", the name still picked out on the front in cobalt blue bottom-heavy seventies font, were the same. I walked up Trafalgar Road and suddenly remembered the cemetery I walked through every day on my way to and from school. It was also identical, and my stomach took another Proustian lurch, the same narrow, overgrown pathways, the small stone buildings and overgrown trees, roots snaking beneath the pathway and breaking up the stones of the graves. One or two shiny black gravestones appeared to be new. I looked at the dates and realised the last time I had walked here these people were alive, perhaps walking through the same cemetery.

I crossed the road into Eastrop Park. A modern bunch of swings and slides appeared bunched together in a corner, as colourful and shifty as the teenagers who smoked mean little fags on them, but almost everywhere else the shittiness and austerity of the park remained intact. A slab-like building, pink as a wafer biscuit, use unknown, remained. The ground was as rough and churned up as it had been when I played abysmal rugby here, shivering, purple-kneed in the snow, unable to touch the cold iron of the ball. I'm not going to romanticise the poverty of my childhood, we always had shoes, if not fruit or *Star Wars* figures.

The not-so-big-any-more hill in Eastrop Park was also the scene of one of my first forays into becoming a human being. As my mum walked me to school, she slipped, hurting her leg. As she sat there wincing with pain, I tugged at her sleeve and whined because I didn't want to be late for school. I spent the rest of the day in a profound depression, contemplating my priorities after failing to live up to the ideals of my hero, Dennis the Menace. I was behaving like a *softy*. Not wanting to miss school? Not wanting to get in to trouble? If Dennis found out, I'd have to return my fan club badge. There was something else, though. Somewhere at the back of my brain was the notion that I was more cowed by authority than I was concerned for my mother's pain. There was something wrong there, something basically flawed. I vowed to change.

I still vow to change.

The library at the end of our road was still there. The prefabricated building, the same three steps leading down from the entrance, the central reservation inside where the librarians lived, all still there. Today's librarian was a cheery chap in specs, but in the past it was a fierce woman who checked you weren't using sleight of hand to take too many books out, as though they were her personal possessions. She stamped them with real violence too, guarding the hairy blue tickets jealously. Children's books were still on the right as you came in. And there was the smell. After thirty-plus years it smelled the same: sawdust and damp, top notes of asbestos.

It was here I discovered books: *Agaton Sax*, *The Eagle of the Ninth*, the *Narnia* series, *The Size Spies*, *Help! I'm a prisoner in a toothpaste factory*, *The Phantom Tollbooth*, *Asterix*, *The Hitchhiker's Guide to the Galaxy*. None of those books are there now. You'd struggle to find a *Bobby Brewster* in a modern library. But the smell was the same. The smell was exactly right.

I headed up to a small bank of shops that I was only ever sent to on half-day closing and always returned empty-handed. Amazingly, it's still there—the same general store where I'd buy the *Beano* and, if I was flush, *Marvel* comics, usually *British Marvel* because they were cheaper and black and white. I got a couple of *Conan the Barbarians* there that were going cheap because they were stained with some sort of yellow liquid. What a lucky fellow, I thought. It was clearly rat's piss. I'm surprised I didn't go blind.

The shop didn't sell comics now. It sold crisps and chocolate and booze. If it wasn't for a couple of tins of soup and a moist loaf of bread, you'd have taken it for an off-licence. There was no natural light in the shop, the windows plastered with posters about bargain alcohol and CCTV, and it had the grim, furtive quality of a sex shop, or the sort of Northern Irish pub that used to have a room for murdering people. I bought a Shandy Bass and left.

Outside a man was sitting down on the ground drinking a Nesquik behind some bins. He said hello and waved his drink. There was a discoloured patch on his grey sweatpants. I waved my Shandy Bass back at him.

I headed down to Easthill Park. I remembered the public toilets. They reeked in high dudgeon, and the summers were always long and scorched then. The smell put me off fish for the first twenty years of my life. On the outside wall, someone had daubed a veiny, ten-foot representation of a phallus, perforated at intervals by safety pins. It bore the legend *Punk Cock* which dated it to 1976 or 1977.

Punk Cock.

Genius.

A man conversed with a young mum while waiting for the barriers to lift outside the train station. He was middle-aged, five foot four and wore glasses, a short white beard and a baseball cap. He would have been easily eliminated in a game of *Guess Who*. The rest of the short distance from his head to his feet was entirely wrapped in sports-leisurewear. A sovereign ring flashed at his knuckle, as he gesticulated and, as he was discussing the paternity of a child, he gesticulated a lot. He maintained he was the child's father as "Ayesha is a dead spit", but it transpired there were two other contenders. One of these was unknown, but the other was Mark Bates. "You know Batesey?" he enquired of the young woman, who happily didn't. "I went after him. We went toe to toe," he claimed. I found it odd that he would refer to a romantic rival and potential father of his child by a nickname, as though Batesey was alright really, he was just being a bit of a dick about the whole paternity thing.

I knew I was naïve. I knew people watched reality television for exactly this sort of window on the world, and it was a long time since I'd been in a relationship, so perhaps that was why I engineered all manner of narratives from this scenario. What was his relationship to the young woman he was confessing this to? Who was the mother of Ayesha, the erotic siren playing these three suitors off one another? What was his relationship with Batesey and what was the outcome of the fight? There wasn't a mark on him so what did Batesey look like? Who was the shadowy third man?

There was a world in this.

The train roared past, the barrier rose hesitantly, and the pair melted into the crowd. I felt judgemental and voyeuristic and deeply sad. This funny little man with his horrible clothes and disregard for personal space, was living a wild, strange, brutal life, fighting and fucking and fathering bastards, right here in my hometown. We might have gone to school together, who could tell at this distance? He might not have gone more than two miles from where he was born his entire life, but he was clearly having a rich and hectic experience, full of pain and joy and noise. My own life was flat, unmarked, and eventless. I had no lovechildren. I hadn't been in a fight since school.

I got on a bus for Hove. The comb-over still reigned in Hove, and an extraordinary example was seated in front of me. It was like a glazed coil-pot propped up on a neck as dusty and wrinkled as an elephant's knee. The hair striped his head in pink and black stripes like something poisonous in nature and contained the sort of structural engineering normally reserved for the roofs of a Victorian railway stations. He clearly went into the barbers with a biography of Isambard Kingdom Brunel tucked under one arm. I missed this. He was like an old man from my childhood. The standard look for your John Bull these days was tattoos, a popped collar, sunglasses and a shaved head, and that was fine, but I preferred a man who injected a bit of mystery into his look. This man's hairy creation had taken a while to get right. There was planning in it. He was risking ridicule just to maintain his own standards. It was joyous.

A distressed gentlewoman got on the bus at Hove station.

"Looks like Minnie Mouse's shoes," she said to one confused passenger, "Your bag—looks like Minnie Mouse's shoes."

She moved on, recognising the woman in the next seat. "Hello," she said.

"Hello," said the woman.

"How are you?"

"I'm fine."

"I'm done with horrible nasty Sue," she said, suddenly savage, "I'm never going to speak to her again and I'm not one bit sorry."

She retreated to a seat next to a woman who flinched and made eye contact with some distant point on the horizon.

"She's a horrible person," she continued, shouting down the bus, "her marriage split up, she had her kids taken away from her and I don't care one bit. She spent thousands on that gown, and I don't give a shit. She's a horrible person."

With this she stopped. The woman in front didn't react. The now silent Sue-hater got off at the next stop. She'd been on the bus for two stops, about 500 yards.

The mobility scooterists travelled in gangs in Hove, like superannuated Hell's Angels, menacing the seagulls. If they had a dog on a leash attached to the scooter, they could take up the same area as a Bedford van. So, of course, they did. The scooters were accessorised with blaring radios, union flags and poppies. Hove wanted no part of Europe with their busy-body rules and footling health and safety mimsyisms. They wanted a Wild West world where they were free to mow people down on pavements without fear of censure. This was why they often wore leather Stetsons. A man looking like Harry Dean Stanton (they were always men, and they all look like Harry Dean Stanton. Men seemed to surrender their legs earlier than women) pelted down the pavement, blaring "Rocks" by Primal Scream. This was surely what Primal Scream intended for that song. The man on the scooter may even have been Bobbie Gillespie, he'd certainly kept the weight off. He looked so happy, so care-free. It was hard to begrudge him his reckless endangerment of my life. Good on you, sir. Wagons roll.

You may have noticed a creeping gerontophobia here. It's hard to criticize the south coast of England for having a lot of old people living in it, given the elderly make up practically the entire population.

I blame Brexit for my prejudice and the, often wrong-headed, notion that all old people voted for it. There did seem to be a lot more flags, poppies and worship of the military around than there used to be, but maybe it was always there, and I just didn't notice. Or maybe it was just me being middle-aged. Teenagers looked gormless and half-formed now, old people were blinkered go-karting idiots, squandering their grandchildren's futures to put Golliwogs back on Robinsons jam labels. Well, I'm wrong. Obviously, I'm wrong. I lost. But I don't feel wrong.

I find the mundane poetry of Southern English place names comforting as the murmur of the sea. As soothing as the Shipping Forecast. Hove, Portslade by Sea, Southwick, Lancing, Goring by Sea, Durrington by Sea, Worthing, Angmering, Ford, ("Welcome to Ford: Home of The Engine Shed") Barnham, Chichester, Southborne, Emsworth, Havant, Warblington, Bedhampton, Cosham, Portchester, Fareham, Swannick, Hamble, Sholing.

Any one of these could be a pal of Bertie Wooster's down the Drones club, or a place where *Dad's Army* went on manoeuvres. It is redolent of shabby gentility, of well-tended gardens with high walls. The houses are small and irreversibly in decline, the owners too old to look after them, young people too poor to afford them. They'll disappear, consumed by the insatiable appetites of property developers until there is nothing left. All those jealously guarded and hard-won little lives eaten up by flats and boutique hotels.

The south coast of England was my first home. But that was a long time ago.

Café de Flaw

I was in a café, writing. I'd given up on the idea of recording the everyday life of common-place folk. I wasn't sure they existed in any meaningful way. I mean, they were on buses or in doctor's waiting rooms, but those weren't really the sorts of places that I wanted to spend time. The waiting room wasn't exactly Café de Flore, and I wasn't likely to philosophise over a tumbler of vin ordinaire with a yellow man who smelled of bandages and couldn't stop shaking. He'd make it all about him. I did wonder about my socialist credentials; I just couldn't seem to get on with the masses. The "Great Unwashed" sounded a bit Victorian and unkind, but it wasn't inaccurate, not really.

I tried writing in a greasy spoon, but they kept asking me to eat fried breakfasts or leave, and old women nudged me and asked me what I was doing.

"I'm writing. I'm a writer."

"Ooh. Have I heard of you?"

It was hard to answer that question without sneering but I really tried.

"No, probably not."

"Are you famous?"

"Well not famous *exactly* . . ."

"Are you that J K Rowlings?"

"No. J K Rowling is a woman."

"Fuck off."
"No. No she is a woman."
"She never fucking is."
"She is. She's a woman."
"All wizards and shit?"
"Yes, even with all the wizards she remains a woman . . ."
"Why?"
"Sorry, could I have my bill please . . ."

I had given up on the general public and now made my way to the sort of coffee shop where they tell you the provenance of each nut without asking if you're interested.

There was one large table in the middle of the room and I was obliged to share it, using my coat as a sort of breakwater. The rest of the seating was at the window, where you could stare out into the street through the steamed glass while perched on a high stool. The floor was concrete, and the walls were grey and bare. Naked light bulbs hung down on flexes like boom mics straying into shot. Fifty per cent of the people were on laptops. The girl opposite me—glasses and one of those hats with ear-flaps—was sketching spectral interior designs into a notebook and referring to a paint chart. She occasionally gnawed on a cake without looking up from her work. The girl next to me wore a bobble-hat and had a visible bra-strap. She had a laptop and a book, but she was fixated on her phone. Behind her were four men grouped around a single table. One of them wore an RAF Flying Jacket, an alpine hat with a feather in the brim, and camouflage trousers flecked with red, so his legs looked like they'd been torn up in crossfire. He wore a thumb-ring and leaned back against the wall, head slightly tilted. The other three, less ornate, more intense, leaned towards him, bent over the table; if they were a band then thumb-ring was the singer. He was talking quietly, and they pushed in to listen to him even as he rested his head against the wall.

A semi-famous comedian sat in the corner of the room looking gym-honed and anonymous in a hoodie. I used to know him before he was even semi-famous, but we didn't acknowledge one another. His hands were folded in front of him, and he had an earnest look, so I assumed he was talking to the man sat opposite him about money.

I was surprised to see that the café staff was all men, but I was more surprised that not all of them had beards. The clean shaven one looked like a young David Cronemberg or Jeffrey Dahmer, if he'd been a bit more socialised. His little teeth were white and perfect; his face was the shape of a foot.

I'd come out specifically to read this room. I wanted to record life as it was lived in the early 21st century. I wanted to make an indelible record of what humans did in what was known as the United Kingdom. You know, like Dickens or Zola or one of the Russian guys would have done. I wanted the grit, the urban squalor, the post-industrial degradation of a superfluous and forgotten metropolitan underclass. Equally though, I wanted a half decent cup of coffee, so the misery was slightly compromised. That was why I was in that café surrounded by young people staring at their phones and conjoined, by the ear, to their laptops. I dearly wanted to know what these they were listening to. But that would've involved talking to them, so it didn't happen.

The coffees on offer were from Guatemala, Ethiopia and, prosaically, Colombia. I plumped for the Guatemalan strain: it was not appreciably different to any other coffee I'd ever tasted. Perhaps a bit stronger.

A demographic sweep of my fellow patrons: 18 people in the room, all but one of them white. Six wore glasses and five had beards. Fourteen of them were men. Four wore enormous scarves. Only one of them wore a hat, as both bobble-hat-bra-strap and flappy-pantone-girl had already left. Five were wearing Dr

Marten's boots and three had Fjallraven back-packs squatting on the bench next to them.

The music was a sort of generic American rock music. It might have been "worthy" and "gritty", had anything survived the Vaseline smear of its production. It was a kind of ersatz rock: if you asked a hyper intelligent computer to create rock music that was slap-bang in the middle of a frighteningly nuanced and sophisticated Venn diagram, then this would be the inoffensive sound emanating from its dead centre. It was music boiled down to its essence—distilled rock. It might have been popular—I wasn't really up on the charts—did they still have the charts? I'd rather lost touch with music since I stopped buying *Mojo* magazine. I got bored of reading about the Beatles. Though it was impressive the way they could keep coming up with fresh perspectives on the same 12 records, month after month, year after year.

I was the only one in the café writing by hand and into a notebook. It must have looked so precious: I might as well have had a wax tablet and a stylus. To them *I* was the hipster, persisting with my archaic nonsense. They were all listening to their own music, headphones plugged into their computers and phones. So, this rock music was for *my* benefit and the benefit of the staff, though they looked none too keen. But who knew? Maybe it was so bad it was good—or maybe it was so *good* it was good or whatever level of densely packed irony we'd reached now. Maybe they just didn't care—the democratisation of music on the internet—everything available all the time—meant they genuinely didn't know the difference anymore. You used to have to have a reason for liking music. There were questions of provenance, of manufacture, of official sanctions from trusted icons. This *mattered* and coloured your perception. It sounds silly now. Being a music enthusiast in those days was like cramming for an exam that never came. Now people treated music like a scented candle, an ambience enhancer, which I suppose it is.

The semi-famous comedian recognised me on the way out and popped over with the glad hand. He was off to do a corporate for an international banking firm for "silly money". It was only a twenty-five-minute set, and he was remarkably sanguine. "To be honest, mate," he said, "the last thing these guys want to do is listen to someone else talk."

He asked me a few perfunctory questions about how I was doing, but his eyes glazed over as I began to answer, and I didn't blame him. Failure is great in an autobiography if it's the starting point or the end point, but a story of unchanging, continuous failure is just depressing. It occurred to me that he had only come over to boast about getting paid, but I was probably being unfair. He waited a good five minutes before even mentioning it—it must have been like sitting on an unscratched itch.

The café counter quietened. There were stacks of paper cups next to black grinding equipment with plastic funnels. There were more cups on top of the giant coffee making machine that resembled a Minimoog made of stainless steel. It looked as though it should have a crumb tray. Next to it were two further anonymous black lumps with Italian name plates fixed to them, all part of the mystery of coffee making: two parts sleight-of-hand to one part disappointment, to one part drawing on the foam. We expect a drawing on our coffee nowadays. Is it like an artist signing their work? My coffee was rich and heavy with a dense burnt chocolate aftertaste. It was a headache in a mug.

This coffee shop sold coffee making equipment. All coffee shops do this now—they're desperate to put themselves out of business. It's like a greengrocer selling you soil and seeds, or a butcher selling you a piglet and empathy suppressants.

I was the oldest person in the café by a good fifteen years. Tell a lie—there was a red-faced businessman in a pale blue tie and one of those colourful Marmot jackets with padded ribs. He had a briefcase, and beneath the table, he was manspreading as though he had just ridden into town on the back of a piping hot bull.

No one spoke. I mean I didn't speak, but I wasn't just staring at my phone, I was clearly engaged in some sort of activity. I'm always wary of falling into the trap of being rude about the younger generation: they could be running million-pound businesses from their phones for all I know, or even doing something useful. Phones are something I find increasingly strange: people's relationships with them have warped beyond all recognition in my lifetime. They used to be doleful Bakelite things squatting in the hallway, and you'd whisper shyly into them whenever anyone walked past. Now they are the entirety of people's lives.

On the bus into town an old woman unfolded a letter from her doctor and had a lengthy conversation, including her vital statistics and her address, over the phone. It was a queasy business but as I looked at the other faces on the bus none of them registered that this was in any way unusual. Just me, then. Just me, the last lonely man.

I was sitting on a school chair. It was exactly the kind of chair I would have sat on at school: the curving pressed wood of the seat and the back support, the splayed gunmetal legs with their rubber stoppers. In the corner, next to the exit, they were stacked next to a fire extinguisher, an exposed concrete pillar, and a steel box control with eight light switches on it. The colour pallet was a symphony in greys. It was a still-life of my school experience; for full synaesthesia you would have to include the thrill of jumping off drama block rostrum and eating grass on a freezing rugby pitch. But the weird industrial grouping worked its magic on me. Who would have thought that twenty years after leaving school I would be paying to drink expensive Guatemalan coffee in a loving recreation of my school dinner hall? All that was missing were the battered pink and blue water jugs, and the distinct tang of nausea.

The café was closing. The baristas were sweeping and placing cellophane over terrine dishes. I looked at my notes. I was still writing a novel about a vampire hypnotist. I had written half a page. Reading it back I decided to score through the entire thing. My uni-ball eye left a smooth wet wake through my afternoon's work. It was the best thing that I had done that day.

I slipped my coat on, and the barista smiled at me and held open the door. I stifled an urge to hug him and went home.

The Playlist of the Gods

I USED TO WRITE in the pub while drinking but found the last couple of pages of anything I wrote difficult to transcribe, as they were blotted with tears and the text comprised largely of angry self-recrimination. I was supposed to be writing a children's book, but it had taken a dark turn.

My favourite pubs are failing concerns: empty, sepulchral bins, the walls plastered with fading memories, boxers with moustaches, fat by today's standards and long dead. Pubs with no one in them. No blaring sport, not even a jukebox, just a settled patina of hopelessness. That's what I need to get the juices flowing.

Now all pubs are awful.

You used to be able to escape from everyday life by going to the pub. No noise, no lights, just the squeak of bar towel on glass and the dropped sand-bag thud of an elderly dog's fart. A pub was an oasis of stolid masculine calm in a screaming metropolitan world. There might be some music played: "Golden Brown" by The Stranglers perhaps, or "Hotel California" by The Eagles, their offbeat time signatures lending the afternoon an unearned air of sophistication. But mostly it had the fusty, clock-ticking, throat clearing ambience of a Gentleman's club, barring the straw on the floor and the challenging toilets.

But now drinking, like everything else, had been colonised by the entertainment industry, and pubs returned to their glittery gin palace beginnings. No longer a man-cave with a late licence, a pub is now a giant neon barn shooting Jägermeister down the gullets of hen parties with t-shirt guns. Pubs are filled with stuffed animals, headless dummies, florescent trees, any amount of detritus salvaged from the skips of the twentieth century, and then nailed to the wall. Sport is always on, bellowing from plasma screens the size of hot hatchbacks.

I was writing in a pub like this. It was a classy version filled with blonde wood shelves and partition walls which had rose-tree and neroli scented candles resting on them. It says they're "rose-tree and neroli" on the bottom of the candles, I couldn't deduce that for myself. I'm not a sommelier of air fresheners. Bare 40-watt bulbs plunged down from the rafters like shower heads. There were old books affixed to the walls, but not flat like a picture in a frame, these books were attached by their spines, jutting out at eye-level, as though laughing in the bleeding face of health and safety legislation.

It was four in the afternoon on a weekday, so mercifully there was no sport on. I bought an ordinary pint of beer (there was a *library* of craft options to be ignored), I whipped out my notebook and sat down.

I was wrestling with what to do with Wainwright, the protagonist of my book. He was a vampire hunter working in modern Belfast and on the trail of the notorious Udo Egerhazi, Count Blutwurst, known to the world as *Count Backwards*, which was also the title of the book. I was pitching it as a Young Adult title because it was exactly the sort of book I would have liked to have read when I was twelve. On top of that I thought the story of a stage-hypnotist vampire might be a bit silly for an adult audience.

It was arrogant, I knew. I'd never bothered to read a Young Adult novel. I hadn't done even basic research. I should have treated it as a proper project: checked out what the key demographic wanted, read selected texts, and worked out the plot, the beats, the character arcs in a classic three act structure. I should have done all the things that they teach you to do in writing classes. But I didn't do any of those things. I just sat down and started writing because I wanted to write about a vampire hypnotist, and I already had the name. And now I was stuck. I was stuck here with my boring hero, Wainwright.

The Count was a delight, as camp as Pontins' tinsel. I could have written him forever. But he had nothing to work against. Wainwright was a bore. That was okay, he was the hero. I liked the idea of a lantern-jawed, old-school hero, who just got his shirt ripped a bit when he got into a fight. I liked his simplicity: you could punch him repeatedly in the face and the only evidence would be a thin trickle of blood coming from the corner of his mouth. There was something wholesome and reassuring about that. But nowadays everything had to be "dark". There's a tyranny of darkness, as though at some point in the '90s a bulb popped, and we've all had to stumble about in the gloom ever since. Everyone is damaged. They're all alcoholics who can't keep a relationship going, or maybe someone they love has been murdered, every last one of them. Why not a detective who's bright eyed? Someone with a spring in his step and who knows how to whistle or shave? The Chirpy Detective. I don't want to relate to him, I can get misery at home. What I want is a brief holiday in someone else's jollity.

The idea of an old-fashioned hero was fine, but I couldn't write him. He was so very boring. The Count was a laugh, but this guy was pissing on his chips, and I just had to stand by and let him do it. The Count had a vision, a plan. He had a raison d'etre. Alright, so a lot of people would end up dying, but come on, people always died when a charismatic man of destiny was up to no good. This Wainwright was a knocker. All he wanted to do was spoil the Count's fun. What sort of a man is motivated by that sort of peevishness? But the main reason I couldn't write for him was because I couldn't focus, and the reason I couldn't focus was the appalling shittiness of the music in the pub.

There were six patrons in the bar: five septuagenarian American tourists and me, and I was confident that none of us were enjoying the music. You've heard this music. It's a kind of American FM punk with suburban lyrics and adenoidal vocals. Variations on it have been around since the mid-90s. It's the soundtrack to white-bread rebellion, anthems for skateboard footage or girls showing their tits in exchange for beads. Its spring-break punk, compressed to fuck like a narrow band of migraine, and it was squeezing my skull like an Italian buying a cantaloupe in the market.

I decided to do something about it. I approached the bar. The bartender was a tattooed man in a flat cap and waistcoat. I couldn't place his age. He was nervy and sinewy and could have been anywhere between thirty and fifty. I find this dishonest. I have the decency to look my age.

"Hi," I said.

"Alright mate." He had small brown eyes, wet as apple pips. They appeared to be processing information about me. I sucked my stomach in.

"You alright?" I said.

"It is what it is," he said, "You know?" I did not know. I'd heard people saying this, but I had no idea what it was meant to convey, beyond some sort of Stoic catchphrase, like the bumper sticker on Marcus Aurelius' chariot. I let it go.

"Pint?" he said.

"No, I've already got a pint. I was wondering if you wouldn't mind turning the music down?"

"Why?"

"Why? Because it's very loud and very bad."

"Yeah," he said, exhaling heavily, "yeah, but there's nothing I can do—its company policy."

"What is?"

"The music."

"It's company policy to alienate your patrons by playing terrible music at them at punishing volume?"

"Yes."

"Okay."

I scanned the bar. There was a laptop perched at the other end. I'd seen him idly scrolling down it minutes before.

"It's only on the laptop. You can't have just one playlist."

"Sorry, mate. That's the company playlist. It's been scientifically compiled for our demographic." I looked at the elderly Americans. They were each bent over the table, gamely attempting to converse, except for one woman who sat back and refused to participate, her arms folded.

"Look, it's just me and the Breakfast Club here. Why not put something else on? They have expensive hearing aids, make it worth their while."

"That's actually pretty ageist?" said the barman, with a rising intonation. He was right. I changed tack.

"Look, what is it? Spotify? I'll knock you up an intergenerational playlist in five minutes, my treat. I used to do a bit of DJing back in the day."

"What day?" said the barman, "D Day?"

"Now who's ageist?" I said, with a grin. I bustled over to the laptop and span it. The playlist was named "Alec's All Killer No Filler Party Hits". Green Day, Blink 182, The Offspring, Sum 41, Avril Lavigne, The Red Hot Chilli Peppers and a dozen other bands I'd never heard of trailed down the screen like liquid shit. The barman sprang at me.

"Don't touch that. That's company property."

"Relax, Alex," I said, "I'm a safe pair of hands."

"Alec," he said, "leave it—you don't work here." But I was already into Spotify and had set up a playlist. First up was "Behind the Smile" by David Coverdale. It doesn't sound like you think it does. It's pretty cool.

"You give it here," said Alec, but I had a full head of steam. I pulled the laptop to the edge of the bar.

"You're not losing anything, Alex, just gaining the respect and admiration of your patrons. And you can't buy that sort of customer relationship."

I typed "My Bag" by Lloyd Cole and the Commotions onto the keyboard, fingers flying. *Mainstream* is far from Lloyd's best album, but that coked up wah-wah driven opener always gets the party started in my house, which tells you about the sorts of parties that get started in my house.

Alec grabbed the computer, but I wasn't letting go as I was about to type "We're Pretty Quick" by The Chob. If you want proper punk, you need to go for the 1960s garage variety, it's the Urtext. The Sex Pistols stole a career. I wrestled the laptop back from him.

"Leave it!" he shouted, as we tussled. "Behind the Smile" began to play, its jerky synth opening failed to win over the Americans, though they had become quite interested in my struggle with the barman.

"See sense, Alex."

"Alec. Let go."

"Just a couple more."

"No. This music's shit."

"You'll never guess who it is? It's David Coverdale from Whitesnake."

"Who?"

"Doesn't it sound like Scott Walker?"

"I've never heard of Scott Walker."

I gasped, and he took advantage of the glancing blow he'd accidentally delivered, wrenching the computer from my hands. It went skidding across the counter, into the air and landed with two soft bounces on the carpet, the screen bent at an awkward angle to the keyboard. *Behind the Smile* came to a sudden and unnatural stop.

There was a frozen moment. Alec and I looked aghast, our faces, our whole bodies, frozen.

"My computer," he screamed, scrambling towards the broken thing.

"You said it was the work's computer."

He turned, teeth bared, a feral animal. I found, to my advantage, that my body worked again, and turned on my heel ready for flight, but Alec, in a sprinting position hurled himself into the vertical with a howl: "You fucking WANKER!"

I saw a sudden, lateral movement from the corner of my eye and Alec seemed to lose traction with the world, his chocolate button eyes widening, his fingers clawing the air as his body dropped, his chin skidding and skinning along the Axminster.

I moved toward my seat to gather up my coat and drain my pint, as Alec turned to face his betrayers, the Americans, particularly the old lady whose leg had crept out and tripped him as quickly as he had attempted pursuit.

"What the fuck?" he queried. The thin foot jabbed at him again.

"There's no need for profanity, young man," she explained, "there are ladies present."

I made a discreet exit, and by the time Alec appeared out of door of the pub I was already on the bus home.

Through a Glass, Barclays

I HAD A DREAM in which someone corrected my pronunciation of the word "reconnoitres". "But I've only ever seen it written down!" I said. The woman in my dream gave me a doubtful look, as though they never stopped reconnoitring down her way. I woke up humiliated and with a huge erection. I had to wait for ten minutes for it to go down before I could have a pee. I can still just about see it, peeping out from beneath my belly, like a pig's nose at the trough.

These days erections are only ever impediments: swelling up when I don't need them like a boil on the back of the neck. I imagine that if I ever actually needed to use one in an erotic context it would be nowhere to be seen, like that vanished tenner you could have sworn you had in your back pocket after a night out; you frisk yourself down but there's nothing there.

I should like to test that absent penis theory one day. I'd dearly like to be proved wrong.

It was a Saturday. I had written quite a bit of my novel *Count Backwards* in the week. I'm thinking Mark Gatiss for the TV version. I've read that TV is the new cinema, that's where the money is, Netflix and whatnot, though I might be getting slightly ahead of myself. Still, I think he'd appreciate the humour.

This week I had also managed to stock the fridge and do the washing up, so I deserved a reward: I was having a dedicated wank day.

One of the good things about living alone (and it's not a long list—knowing the provenance of every pube on the bathroom floor might be the only other entry) is that I can masturbate whenever I feel like it.

As Woody Allen once said . . . well, you can't really quote Woody Allen anymore. Probably best not to get started. But I would say that everything we know about Woody Allen, everything he's said and everything he's done, would indicate that he is an enthusiastic celebrant of masturbation. And who can blame him. It's just the best.

Contrary to the findings of Victorian pseudo-scientists and their bondage pyjamas, masturbation is a healthy, natural and invigorating pursuit. And as a middle-aged man who owns a car and lives alone, it constitutes the only regular exercise I get.

I belong to a gym. It's part of a package with work and I do go through binges of exercising, often when I'm feeling more than usually morose about being single. It doesn't seem to make any difference—I fear I'm a write-off. There is a sort of cosmic unfairness. I was skinny until I was thirty. I was known for it—"Skinny Paul" they used to call me. My friends weren't in the first rank when it came to thinking up nicknames. I could go out, drink ten pints, get a kebab on my way home, sit on my arse in an office all week and do the same the next weekend and never gain a pound.

Now I could go to the gym three times a week, give up drinking, eat steamed kale for breakfast, lunch and dinner and never sweat an ounce. It's discouraging. I feel like one of those chronically poor people who can't pay their rent, but they buy a takeaway anyway. They're in debt either way so they might as well stuff their faces. And that's how thin people look at me—as if it was all my fault. But it's only partially my fault. My parents were perfectly spherical for as long as I knew them. We'd walk down the street together when I was younger, and we'd look like the number 100 (or the word "loo" if you want to be lower case about it). It was always there, lurking in the genes. I was born a latent sphere and a sphere I have become.

I'm exaggerating. I still look thin unless you see me in profile. My weight sits squarely on the tight rubber ball of my belly. I can wear a cardigan or a big coat to disguise it. If I'm on a date I try to engineer a situation where I can spend the entire evening face-on, like an erotic newsreader, in complete denial of my third dimension. I don't get many second dates, but usually that's a relief. If the object of dating is ultimately to confront someone with your naked body, I probably shouldn't be trying.

My ideal situation would be a relationship where the woman was always naked, and I was always fully clothed. Obviously, this is a fantasy—in real life it would not only be impractical but disturbing. What's the nature of this relationship? Is she manacled to anything? Why doesn't she ever go out? I need some *me* time. Who's paying those heating bills? She's stifling me in more ways than one. It's just not going to work.

And then I remember it's not real. Calm down. Have a cup of chamomile tea. Bloody hell.

It was a bright sunny day and so I half drew the curtains and fired up the laptop. There are a few websites I frequent, and I pull them all up so that I can flit between them—keep things fresh, you know? They have clever modern algorithms now so the pornography I am greeted with reflects my preferences. It doesn't look good. When you're down a pornographic rabbit-hole you will look at some strange, strange stuff. It's like a black box for the id. There will be a clause in my will to have my laptop incinerated on the occasion of my death. Assuming there is anyone to act on my behalf. I'm not sure it's covered by my Over-Fifty's life insurance.

One of the things about being bone-deep lonely is staying awake at night fretting over who will destroy my laptop when I'm gone. But I *am* lonely. I'm *so* lonely. So, I look at pornography.

I'm being disingenuous—I've been in relationships before, and it didn't stop me looking at pornography. I just really, really like the look of naked women. And it's the best place to spot them, especially in my flat. I'm not saying I wasn't lonely in those relationships, but at least I had somebody to hide the pornography from, which was not only an illicit thrill but an effort. I used to like making an effort and having someone to make an effort for. I missed washing my clothes, cleaning my body, being obliged to do things I didn't want to do. I miss meeting my partner's friends whom I didn't like. You never know what you're going to miss.

I have literally nothing to do today. I have no appointments, no social engagements, no reason to leave the house. So, I'm going to sit on the sofa and look at naked people doing things to one another. I could do some writing, but I've done quite a lot this week.

This is my reward.

Naked women fill the screen of my computer. Well, they're not women—they're girls. They could be my daughter, though they are far too good looking.

Pornography is tricky. As I say, I like looking at naked women. I really like the shape, the young, taut skin. I used to like it in real life too but that's not going to happen now. Sorry, it's not just the skin—I'm not a serial killer. I like the whole package, eyes, teeth, hair, whatever. But you can only *see* those, and that's all you can ever do. You can touch skin, feel its softness, its smoothness, the way it cleaves to the bone, the gentle recoil of its elasticity, its heat . . . and we're back to serial killer territory again.

I don't necessarily approve of pornography but it's hard to consider ethical questions with your trousers round your ankles.

I gather my equipment about me. It's just stuff to clean me up afterwards. I'm not into the kinky shit. And I unbuckle my belt. My penis rests on my thigh, unstirring. A child under a duvet on a winter's school day. The girls on the screen go through their contortions, gymnastics' loss is my gain, but nothing happens. I shake the penis. It's like a boxer out for the count—I may need a bucket of water. I stare at it. It lies there, naked as something peeled from its shell. Maybe the pornography is wrong. I switch to another site and grip my penis with fresh urgency—shaking hands with the unemployed, my friend Brendan calls it, and he should know. I attempt to build up a rhythm. The girl on screen is particularly limber, dark skinned, slender as a shadow, a long nose, thick, dark hair.

Nothing.

My shoulders hunch. I'm waving my penis between thumb and fore-finger now, describing a smooth arc like a flaccid wind-screen wiper. The camera pans down the girl's body to reveal that she too has a penis. A larger one than mine. She has uncoiled it from her G-string, where it must have been packed in like a Cumberland sausage. And my cock wakes. Like a flower sensing the first rays of the sun it slowly reveals itself, jack-knifing in increments towards my belly button. What does this mean? This rude awakening has come a bit late in the day. Am I gay now? At my age I can't get a heterosexual woman. What chance would I stand with a gay man? I'm Methuselah in gay years. I'm Jurassic pork. I'm all for gender fluidity when you're young—knock yourselves out lithe, hairless Gen Z, but I'm set in my ways about my breakfast cereals, never mind the other. Still, perhaps my penis disagrees, the cock is deceitful above all things, and my hand continues to work away despite the furious re-calibrations going on in my mind.

I'm so consumed by this fifty/fifty division of blood flow, that I don't hear it at first. Outside the house is the twitching of rubber hoses being uncoiled, the muffled braggadocio of young men, and the rustle of their sportswear. There is the metallic groan of ladders being unlocked, extended.

Something hits the window with a slap at the exact moment I ejaculate, and for a moment I conflate these two events and stare in confusion and panic at the window. Could I have...? But it's about nine feet...?

A second thud on the windowpane, and a fat sponge exudes suds as it squeaks across the glass.

Window cleaners.

Panicking, I stare up at the half-closed curtains. The sponge is already peeking around them. How long until a window cleaner follows it, until he reaches clear glass—this is a ground-floor flat.

I leap up from the sofa forgetting that I'm manacled at the ankles by trousers and pants and topple over like a felled tree, arms splayed out in front of me. And this is what the window cleaner sees as he finally moves past the curtains: me, bare arsed on the carpet, my arms stretched out in front of me as though swimming lengths of the living room. I can hear his laughter through the glass and decide that I will just lie there as damage limitation, and finally spent, he will retreat to his van and I can cover up my cock and balls at my leisure. Then I'll write a note telling him that from now on I'll leave the money under the doormat, and we'll never need to talk to one another again. Perfect.

I lay there and eventually the laughter stopped. But the man didn't go away, and I could hear a second, deeper voice, full of consternation. There was a loud rap at the window. I froze. Oh God, *just go away*. But they were not going—they were shouting. More raps on the slick glass. Oh Christ, please. Stop tormenting me. The banging stopped. The voices went away. I waited.

Finally.

I shifted around like a landed fish. There was no sign of them at the window. I pulled my knees up, arse in the air when there was a loud crashing at the door and the splintering of wood and two large men in baseball caps flooded into the room.

"What the fuck?" I said.

"Don't worry, mate," said the older of the two, my age, "we've got you. We've called an ambulance."

The other one grabbed me under the armpits. He still had a fag in his mouth.

"What are you doing?" said the older man. "Let the ambulance sort him. Leave him alone."

"We can't leave him lying on the floor."

"You have to, you might . . . disturb something if you shift him."

"What'd we break the door in for then?"

There was a pause.

"Let's get him on the sofa."

I went along with this as I was already so incapacitated by shame that my body had completely shut down. Perhaps I could pretend to be narcoleptic. I might even keep up the charade for the ambulance crew when they arrived. I'd take my chances with an undertaker.

They put me on the couch and the older one places a cushion over my glistening genitals.

"There you go, old son."

There's a sudden shrill cry from the laptop, the sound of a woman, a woman with a penis, reaching the summit of her ecstasy, pretty much the exact opposite of what I was feeling at that moment.

The penny dropped for the window cleaners. The older one stood over me shaking his head. I maintained close scrutiny of the carpet.

"I told you," said the younger one.

"Disgusting," said the other, "it's the middle of the afternoon."

"It's a Saturday," I said in a low monotone, refusing to look up. The older one sucked his teeth.

"C'mon, let's go," he said, and they slipped from the living room and out through the ruined door into the street outside. I could hear equipment being moved, and presently the sound of a van driving off. I wondered if I could afford to buy a new door or pay a man to fix the existing one. I wondered what I would say had happened to the upstairs tenant. I wondered where I could get a doormat. I looked at the deep blue of the sky beyond the cloud bank of soap suds on the glass. It was a beautiful day. I pulled my trousers up and waited for the ambulance.

It's the Most Wonderful Time of the Year

I'M IN ANOTHER QUEUE for another coffee shop. There are two members of staff working and one other person in the queue. He's a charming old duffer—long and spare, immaculately turned out in an expensive scarf and cap combination. He's wearing boat shoes, though we are some miles from the nearest marina. I glance into the street to see where he's parked his yacht, but there's no sign of it. I hope it hasn't been towed away by the coastguard. He's talking about his family to the female member of staff who looks rapt. She's pretty, with a round face and brown, smiling eyes. She answers his questions in broken English. She may be Italian, or she might be from somewhere in Eastern Europe, I can't tell. I hear Polish people on the bus and think they're French. The rhythm of the language is similar, or something.

The other server is a doughy bearded bloke with a side-parting. He is engaged in the actual making of the coffee, she's obviously more customer liaison.

"You over here to see your family?" she says. Not to me.

"Yes, yes, I have family here," says the duffer. He doesn't get the wallet out and flash the baby photos, but it's touch-and-go for a moment.

"Soon it is Christmas. You have to do it all over again." She bursts into laughter at this, and I want her to talk to me and laugh at the unfunny facts of my life with the same joy. I am immediately in love with her.

"Yes, Christmas," says the man, "you know, family, friends . . . Christmas . . ."

"Turkey!" she explodes. He laughs along with her, and I also smile as if I'm in on the joke, if only someone would look at me. I came in for a coffee, but I find instead I am eavesdropping on inane pleasantries and trying to prove to a pretty girl that I'm a nice man, just in case she wants to make me a coffee, which I would pay for because it's a café after all, and that is what's supposed to happen.

I look around. Uninspiring cakes sit in glass cabinets. There are chiller shelves of microwavable sandwiches and wraps. Christmas bunting in the colours of the café's corporate branding twist between glass jars. Fairy lights flash blue and white. The light is an ambiance killing glare, and the floor is the sort of wood laminate that sounds like a gunshot if you drop a fork on it. It was not an auspicious venue for literary creation.

The bearded boy finally finished making the coffee and handed it over to the old man. "Any sugar?" "No, no sugar," said the old man and the girl laughed again, as though he'd said, "I'm sweet enough," or some such quip. But no, he just declined the sugar and it'd brought the house down. He strutted off in his expensive knitwear like he'd just smashed it at an open mic night.

"Alright, mate," said the boy to me. His voice was light and soft and another voice, distinctly like my father's, chimed at the back of my head with the word "poof". I smothered that voice by horribly over-compensating.

"Alright mate, how are you?" I beamed, looking him in the eye in a manner that was confident, friendly and not at all concerned as to whether he'd washed his hands since his last toilet assignation, if they still did that, though I don't know why they'd bother since they're *everywhere* now, even kids' TV, *especially* kids' TV. They probably do still meet up in toilets just for the kinky thrill of it and who am I to judge? I haven't had a kinky thrill since the pole tax riots. I couldn't see this one as a toilet trader, though. He was chubby and hairy, not gym toned and intense. There were no visible tattoos and his eyebrows looked untouched by human hand, so I don't think he was a "scene" gay. Do they still say "scene"? Do that still say "gay"? I'll have to ask Neil at work. He is my "go-to" gay. Although I don't like Neil. Not cause he's gay, but because he's a little shit.

While I was thinking about this the server either ignored or answered my question and was now waiting for my order. The pretty girl had disappeared. I ordered a cappuccino, and he made it without any chat. I paid with a twenty-pound note and he gave me change in coins, even though it was 6.30 at night and the shop had been open since ten that morning.

I ferried the coffee over to a table, sat down and took out my notebook, pen and phone.

A big fat man with a silver quiff and glasses waddled up to the counter. He had an anorak, a man-bag and a newspaper which was folded under his arm but looked suspiciously like the Daily Mail. And suddenly the girl was back, eyes dazzling, shooting-the-shit with this absolute bollock of a man. I looked on in quiet fury to see what kind of change he would get at the end of the transaction, but he paid with a fiver, so I was unable to draw any reasonable conclusions.

I started to write a new scene: Wainwright, the tedious bore I had lumbered myself with as the hero of my book, was meeting the vampire Udo Egerhazi's niece in the garden of a nice country pub. It was artistic licence as the main body of the story is set in Belfast and there are no nice country pubs in Belfast. There are no decent pubs of any stripe at all in Belfast. The locals will tell you there are, and they'll recommend them to you using words like "authentic" and "proper", and then take you to some dismal barn full of shrieking harpies and fat elbowed farmers in checked shirts, a freezing shed where you can't get a seat or get near the bar. "Great buzz about the place, so there is," they'll say as you stand shivering in your coat staring at the collection of vintage tea trays nailed to the wall. They'll tell you the fish and chips are good too. They don't know what they're talking about.

I couldn't write. Something was bothering me. Something somebody had said. I stared out the window. It was dark. People walked past wrapped up in their puffy jackets and colourful sweaters, carrying shopping bags filled with green and red tat.

Christmas. It would be Christmas in three weeks, the girl had said so. Christmas was coming.

I like to imagine that Christmas is the sort of thing that only happens to other people, but there's no avoiding it. Christmas happens to you whether you want it to or not. I have no family. I have few friends and the ones I do have are precious little comfort. The TV is already full of rosy-cheeked children and cosy sweaters and that sort of twinkle-eyed schmaltz the American's imagine they excel in, and which only serves to alienate the rest of the world. I've never been to America, and I know now that I never will go—even though a return flight to New York is now cheaper than a rail journey between London and Manchester. America is a violent circus, a moronocracy. I hope they *do* build a wall, just to keep all the bastards in. None of them have passports anyway, guns but no passports. Those fat dozy fuckers grinning at World Heritage Sites in matching cagoules, claiming to be related to everyone in sight, are the savviest, most cosmopolitan members of the population: they're what the Daily Mail likes to call "The Cultural Elite". God help us all. Build the wall, seal it up and whatever crawls out in fifty years gets to be President.

Americans aren't really the enemy, but they *have* sort of colonised Christmas. It's an event now immortalised by the appearance of a heavy goods vehicle full of cans of sticky, tooth-rotting pop, and the notion that "holidays are coming". Well, for one thing it used to be a single holiday—12 days is nearly two weeks, and that's long enough for most people. Now the trees are up on the first of December and Channel 5 is screening Hallmark comedies about hard-nosed businesswomen learning to love again underneath the holly jolly mistletoe from mid-November. Also, do they even have holidays in America? I thought that taking the day off work was rather frowned upon, like free medical care or not shooting black people in the face.

Christmas is a difficult time. I usually feel okay about being alone but, and I know it's very dull and obvious, not at Christmas. Christmas is a time that exacerbates my misery to an unbearable degree. I am very much not looking forward to it. I don't have a tree. What would be the point? No one would see it but me. If you strip away the tinsel, baubles and fairy-lights you're left with a tree sat in your house, shedding. There is nothing under it but dropped pins. I received no gifts barring the Secret Santa one from work, and last year it was a pair of fluffy handcuffs and some lube, which was obviously hilarious because they all know I'm single. And well outside the agreed tenner price range—it was high-end, name-brand lube. I'm looking at you, Neil.

Instead of working on the book, I look around, hoping to at least get a bit of local colour: a bumptious Dickensian oaf or a sixties Parisian gamine. But these prove to be ambitious ideas. There are a couple of students, a couple of businessmen with laptops, nicely attired middle-aged women sat in the window. They aren't middle aged—I'm middle aged—they're in their sixties, which used to be old. But these women look great in their scarves and expensively coiffed hair. One of them is wearing jeans and I note, as she goes to the toilet, her arse isn't half bad. Better than mine, certainly.

A family walks by on the other side of the road, no doubt Christmas shopping. The parents are in their early thirties: him dark, her blonde. She's pushing a buggy and is clearly carrying child number two. He has the lead of a Labrador in one hand and a shopping bag in the other. They're each wrapped up in understated, though expensive looking, leisurewear. Their curly haired moppet of a child is a dear. They don't look quite real. They look like an advertising agency's idea of a family; they should be talking about changing their boiler or taking out an insurance policy for the price of a cup of coffee per week. But there they are: parading their hyper-normality on the streets, their magical ordinariness.

And here I am looking for a crumb of affection from a barista who is just trying to do her job and writing longhand a novel about a hypnotist vampire. In a fit of shame, I close the notebook and snatch up the pen and my phone, punching my way into the sleeves of my coat.

As I stride toward the door, already thinking of rewarding/punishing myself with a bottle of bottom-shelf red, I hear a voice: "Thank you. Bye."

I turn and see it's the pretty barista, standing there beaming with a mop in her hand. I don't know what my face is doing in the half a second or so that I point it at her, but it is enough to make the smile melt away like the froth on a latte.

I pop my collar and scuttle off like Nosferatu in search of an off-licence, calculating exactly how long it will be before I can return to this café. I'm running out of them.

Fanfare for the Gammon Man

The day had not gone well, not really. I'd been sending out preliminary chapters of my novel, *Count Backwards*, to publishers. Normally this is like opening the window and fucking the night, my tiny silken string lost instantly in the darkness. My work, and by extension myself, are not worth anybody's consideration. Writers complain that what they are now required to produce is not writing but *content*. I am beneath content.

There is something almost pleasurable about firing off your precious work into the velvety embrace of the void, all that comfortable emptiness: an unsullied, pristine nothing. It's like sending Voyager off into space and knowing that it's still out there, insignificant and lost, shrugged off the shoulder of Orion. Being continually ignored was, initially, damaging to my ego. Not knowing if the work had ever been read or even made it into the foothills of somebody's slush pile was depressing. But I'd relaxed over time. What did I care? It was rare that I even sent physical copies these days, so it wasn't even costing me postage. It was just the matter of a quick bit of research to find the correct name, a bit of tailoring on the template letter and then pressing send. And I would never hear from them again.

Except today. Today I'd had two replies.

The first was a polite and brief e-mail: *Count Backwards* was not right for their list. They sent their apologies. Normally there would be a line about my writing showing merit but that had been excised.

The other was a letter sent to my work address from a publisher I'd never heard of. I must have sent them a manuscript or pages some time ago, but I couldn't remember anything about them. The editor, a woman named Amanda, had been quite thorough. The premise of the book—a vampire hypnotist living in Belfast—was dismissed as "sophomoric and confused" and my writing style was "frustratingly pedantic and littered with misplaced or unnecessary semi-colons".

Fine.

Her opinion.

My characters were both "poorly drawn and grotesquely melodramatic". Actually, thank you! That was a compliment! It was meant to have a *Boy's Own*, Grand Guignol quality. There was "a dearth of interesting female characters". Yeah, I'll give her that. There was *one* female character, the hero's love interest and latterly a snack for the vampire. I had momentarily forgotten her name, which I suppose rather proved Amanda's point, so one nil to her.

In her summing up, and she had the manner of a bumptious barrister approaching climax. She crowed: "Frankly, the MS as it stands displays no attempt to meet the current Young Adult market. The book is reactionary, violent, woefully sexist and wholly sexless. It investigates no issues and, when it intersects with real life at all, it seems entirely coincidental or prosaically mundane. There is the *germ* of a good idea here, but it is being drowned by the 'Domestos' of your prose! (Good one) The worst thing is that it's so old fashioned: it's like a book from the '60s or '70s. My advice to you if you want to work in the Young Adult genre is to *actually* read some Young Adult fiction, because at the moment you sound less Young Adult and more Decrepit Pensioner." No further questions, your honour, no further questions!

At the bottom she added "I'm sorry I couldn't be more positive" which as a parting-shot was perfectly judged.

I'd read the letter several times while sitting on the toilet at work. Later, standing at the bus stop, I fished it out of my pocket and started looking at it again. I was thinking up a few pithy one-liners for an e-mail I would never send, when I became aware of a disturbance. At the far end of the bus stop a fight had broken out between two young people. It had crept up on me, as I was once again poking about in the guts of the letter, but now I heard it, shrill and harsh, the guttural consonants hissed out, flint hard onto the pavement. There was a girl, small and thin with long red hair and blueish skin which bruised to purple at her nose. Her lips were large and red and tightly framed her sharp white teeth. She'd been straddling a boy, facing him as he sat on the bench. He was skinny and tattooed with a sulky mouth and deep-set eyes. They'd initially been embracing but now he held her firmly by the wrists as she struggled to get to her feet.

"I can't believe you," she said, "I can't fucking believe!"

"Don't be stupid," he said, "you're being stupid."

"Don't call me stupid," she spat, "I'm not fucking stupid."

"Don't fucking swear," he said, "I fucking hate it when you swear!"

"Stop fucking making me fucking swear then!" she screamed, and he let go of her wrists and she fell backwards onto the pavement, slapping it with sudden violence. She sat there wide-eyed and panicked.

"What the actual fuck?" she squealed.

He was on his feet now, fists balled by his hips, bent over her. His body was taut, clenched. I didn't know what was going to happen next. My hackles had been up since the moment their raised voices penetrated my self-absorption. I'd squirmed to the farthest end of the bench, stomach churning. My body hair was uselessly on end. A gentle slick of perspiration flooded my inlets and my tongue felt air-dried, like a chicken in a Chinese shop window.

"Come on then!" she said.

Oh bloody hell.

"Come on then, you prick!"

Oh Christ.

I got to my feet. My last interaction with young people hadn't gone well. I'd been racist on a bus. A boy had been trying to return my wallet which I'd dropped on the floor and I'd assumed he was going to stab me. It was embarrassing, really. This was an opportunity to make amends. If I could broker peace between these warring children then perhaps it could go some way towards making up for it. I was disappointed neither of them was black, but the boy could have been Asian or something and that was nearly as good.

"Guys," I said, as though I was about to ask them if they'd had a chance to look at the specials menu, "Guys, c'mon. What's all this about?"

"Fuck off, Granddad," said the boy.

"Woah!" I said, "I'm 56, mate!"

"My Nan's 49," he said.

"Really?" I said, judging her quietly. "C'mon, why don't you pick her up. There's no need for all this."

He turned to me. He was short and wiry, and tendons stood out at the side of his neck. He moved like a robot, his limbs stiff with fury.

"What's it got to do with you?"

"Well," I said, "there's a social contract . . ."

"There's a fucking what?"

"A social contract . . ." I said again, the words pot pourri in my throat.

"Fucking hit him, Daisy!" said the girl. I shot her a quick disappointed look before he punched me in the face. I went down immediately. My fighting style has long been to play dead and hope my assailant runs away thinking he's killed me. She was immediately on her feet, giving me soft, exploratory kicks.

"Get up," she said, "get up."

I lay there, not saying anything. I wasn't sure what my next move should be.

"Fuckin' get up," she said, with another quick, light kick to my back.

"Baby," said the boy, "please don't swear."

"Kick him, Daisy."

Wait a minute—Daisy?

"Is your name Daisy?" I said to the boy.

"What's it to you?" he said, defensively. It was a foolish line of enquiry, I knew, but I couldn't help myself.

"Daisy? Like the flower? Like a cow would be called?"

"Kick him, Daisy," said the girl, with a note of tension in her voice. I was a fat middle-aged man who had been decked by her boyfriend with a single punch, but at least I wasn't called Daisy and she must have known that. His prestige was slipping.

"You looking for a kicking, mate?" said Daisy.

"I don't know, Daisy," I said, "you going to use your 'daisy roots'?"

"You what?"

"Daisy roots—it's cockney rhyming slang for boots. Seriously, no one knows anything anymore. I mean, I know you're wearing trainers, but I was stretching a point..."

He kicked me. It wasn't like one of the girl's feathery punts. He measured it, skipped back a step and took a well-balanced and balletic lunge, catching me square in the stomach, and neatly dispersing my internal organs like a decent snooker break. I lurched forward, retching, breathless. No air seemed to be coming in or out of me, while my guts settled like muesli in transit. I braced myself against the bench, eyes bulging, still feeling the slow reverberation of the hot meat of my body. I wondered if I would ever breathe again. In the haze of my peripheral vision, I noticed the boy hanging back to see what would happen next, while his girlfriend advised him to finish the job.

My guts righted themselves and breath flooded my body again with a low groan. I attempted to stand, one hand on the bench the other held out in front of me.

"Look, he's fine," said the girls voice, "hit him again."

"Fuck you think you're doing?" said another voice, old and coarse and with real venom. An old woman appeared as I continued to drool and groan. She was about four foot nine, wore jeans and a large cardigan and had long grey hair. Her arms were folded across her chest, and she had a cigarette in her right hand. "The fuck you think you're doing. Leave him the fuck alone."

"What's it got to do with you?" said the girl, but you could tell her heart wasn't in it. Already the boy had a defensive arm around her and was ushering her away.

"He's a poor old man. Leave him the fuck alone. What's wrong with you?"

Old man? How old was she? She looked about seventy. The cheek of it.

"Go on. Fuck off out of it," she cried after the retreating couple.

"Alright, alright," said Daisy, "Women round here got seriously nasty mouths on them. It's un-fucking-couth." They bickered off into the night.

Having dragged myself to my feet, I wiped the saliva from my lips with my sleeve. The woman had a small pink face like a Troll doll, and one of those flat noses I associated with hereditary drunks. There was a ring on every finger. She appraised me with tiny, bright eyes.

"Thank you so much," I said.

"It was fucking stupid what you did. You're why people get themselves killed."

"You're probably right, but . . ."

"You could be dead. You weren't no match for him. He's a young man." She wasn't leaving it alone.

"No," I said.

"You'd barely be a match for me."

I looked her up and down.

"I think I could take *you*," I said.

"Yeah, I saw how you handled yourself. Like a sack of shit." Her chin was tilting up and she was smoking at me now.

"Thanks for all your help but you can go now. I'd appreciate it if you would just leave me to my bleeding."

A bus pulled around the corner.

"There's your bus," she said.

"Thank you, but I'd sooner walk."

I walked off into the night, not entirely sure where I was. The palms of my hands were grazed, and I could smell/taste thick copper blood. That was the price you paid for being a white knight. Chivalry had taken a kicking tonight. I was trying to be an ally and the girl had immediately turned on me. I had threatened the pair of them, threatened the fractious status quo of their relationship. She was angry with my attempts to come between them. I wish I had somebody who loved me like that. Well, not like that—that was awful. But I wish I had someone who loved me like *something*.

I walked only as far as the next bus stop and sat down, peeling the lacy frills of skin from my palms. The next bus was in twelve minutes and the off-licence would be shut, but I had a bottle of Grand Marnier at the back of the cupboard left over from the Christmas before last. I decided that work tomorrow was going to be a struggle.

Spruces Rough in the Distant Glitter

I WAS EATING some toast and scrolling through social media, when I noticed I'd been tagged in a photo. As a middle-aged man I do not post on social media. I patrol it and offer the benefit of my wisdom when I notice a serious infraction of logic, before moving on. The picture I'd been tagged in was from work's Christmas party. I failed to recognise myself.

I do occasionally take a selfie. My selfies are taken at a specific angle. You know the one: from above, accentuating the eyes and minimising the fallout of wattles and chins. I still look alright from that angle: unsmiling, in grainy black and white. I look like the bass player from a minor indie band photographed for the Melody Maker in 1988, and I'm very happy with that. In fact, I *was* the bass player of a minor indie band in 1988. But when I'm tagged in someone else's photo what I most frequently resemble is Christopher Biggins, backstage at the Palladium, and surprised in the act of climbing into his Widow Twankey costume. I clicked on this link. It didn't disappoint.

My face was not featured. Instead, the side view of a belly, clearly mine as I recognised the cardigan, had been taken unawares. In the distance, using clever forced perspective, I could see Neil from the office, smirking and apparently resting his pint on the swell of my belly. It was artfully done and quietly devastating. I'd no idea how far my belly had gone. I'd been living in a fool's paradise of big coats and duck-faced photos, but here was the truth, hard and round and pressed into my belt buckle. I'd been publicly shamed. My face wasn't in the picture, but my guts had been tagged, and my name ran across my stomach as though I was wearing my own merchandise. I looked like one of those mad Californian dads-to-be who stick pillows up their jumpers trying to understand what their pregnant partners are going through. Maybe just ask them, yeah?

This was a clear sign: either I would have to eat better food, drink less and do more exercise, or I would die. I would die *anyway*, but I didn't want to be buried in a piano-crate lowered into the ground by a JCB and painted black as befitted the solemn occasion.

I was a member of a gym, but I hadn't been back after my induction, where a serious young woman explained the use of the apparatus to me with impressive economy. I later saw her laughing and joking with a muscular man with a tattoo of a scorpion on his calf. He was leaning over her at the vending machine as she sucked on an isotonic sports drink. I assumed they were laughing at me, so I didn't go back, though that wasn't the only reason. I was too unfit for the gym. I needed to work my way up to the gym. I wasn't about to collapse, sprawling and puce on one of the running machines, my leg locked in cramp like rigor mortis.

I'd go for a walk. I was a man whose leisure hours were chiefly filled with drinking, masturbating and listening to records. If I opened the curtains it was a good day. I would go for a walk, breathe some fresh air, harvest some vitamin D. This was a good idea. Fuck Neil. I would turn his spite on its head. He'd unwittingly been an agent for change in my life. I opened the curtains. It was a bright sunny day. I immediately started sneezing.

Stepping outside, the sky was blue, the streets empty, the air cold and pure. I wasn't wearing sportswear. I have some, somewhere, but this was just a walk, not an Iron Man competition, and besides what if I met a woman. Even though it never happened, it was always at the back of my mind, and if opportunity knocked I didn't want to be wearing tracksuit bottoms, a faded Faust t-shirt and a pink cummerbund of sagging belly flesh. No. I put on my oldest and most comfortable shoes, my shiniest raincoat, slipped my headphones over my ears and stepped out of the flat. Grace Jones' version of "La Vie En Rose" brightened an already shiny day, its taut acoustic guitar sparking over rubber-band bass. My cheeks were kissed pink by the crisp morning air. I felt good. Goodish.

Near my house is an abandoned railway line, a victim of Dr Beeching's enthusiastic surgery in the 1960s. It had been cemented over and was now a place for dog walkers and cyclists, and the trees on either side grew tall and dark. According to a sign there were three species of bat living there though I'd never seen any. The pathway was a slalom of dog shit, with most of the individual turds bisected by tyre or tread marks. It was old people, of course. Old people didn't pick up their dog's waste. They never had to before and they weren't about to now, just because some Herbert from the council told them they should. I can see their point, bending over to pick up a sandwich bag full of faeces when you might never straighten up again seems like a fool's errand. And they do love their furry little friends, they'd be so lonely without them. Maybe I should get a dog, because I feel your pain old people, I am fucking lonely. But, by the same token, pick up little Benjy's crap. It's disgusting.

Beneath the canopy of trees, I kept exact time with "Magic Fly" by Space, the helmet-wearing disco Frenchmen. The path made a definite incline and weaved nimbly through the trees, and I wondered how a train would have been able to negotiate this trail. You forgot about the path's provenance until you reached an abandoned station where slabs of concrete pushed through the foliage. Look upon my works ye mighty, in disrepair.

These stops must have been rudimentary affairs even when they were in use: a third of the length of a train and no roof in evidence, just the bare cement platform carpeted by moss and tagged over again and again, a blank slate to be endlessly rewritten. I stared at the incoherent glossolalia and one word peeped through, faded from its original acid chrome yellow: "Parp". I had no idea if that was someone's name or some sort of youth slang or if it meant what I thought it meant and someone, for their own reasons, had decided to paint the word "parp" onto a sleeper in a defunct train station. I don't suppose I'll ever understand art.

I carried on up the hill, my pace dictated by The Walker Brothers' "Nite Flites". I found the plodding drumming quite effective on the flat, but against the incline it became a struggle.

Once I reached the brow of the hill the landscape changed completely. The trees were cut back and there were redbrick walls either side of me. I found myself on a bridge over-looking a motorway. The cars had their headlamps on even though it was three in the afternoon. The sky was now white and sunless. A raw wind blew across the newly exposed pathway, and I felt a drop of rain on my forehead. I pressed on across the bridge. It wasn't rain. It was snow. A sudden heavy flurry of snow came from nowhere, and pressed against me, sticky as rice, covering my coat in fat heavy flakes. I could feel the snow settle on my eyelashes as I moved on into the tumult, the path ahead a soft, white tunnel, the snow dancing like scratches on film.

"Fuck this," I thought, and turned back the way I'd come so the wind was behind me, but the snow had started to settle, and the rubbery swell of the concrete pathway was slippery underfoot. I stepped forward, but the earth moved beneath me, the tread of my old shoes frictionless. I slipped and landed wet-arsed with a slap. I sat on the empty pathway with no idea which way to turn, into the blind eye of the storm or inching along the way I'd come on my backside, clinging to tree roots and pieces of protruding masonry.

I was as far from home as my planned journey would take me. I was stranded at the exact point of equidistance.

On the other side of the bridge, steps led down to a small shopping village: a Co-Op, a pub, a launderette, a Libyan restaurant (quite nice, actually). More specifically there were roads. I could call a taxi, get collected.

I fished my phone out of my pocket to dial Local Cabs, my local cab company. The phone was immediately wadded in thick snow, but I managed to phone the number.

Engaged.

Fine.

I should have gone to the pub and had a pint and waited for the storm to blow over. But I'd never liked the look of that pub. It was like a glorified home bar, like something from 1980s Essex: "Lee's Bar" written on it in Letraset, while mein host rattles the ice for a Tom Collins, his teeth glinting through his blonde moustache.

I have a rule about pubs. I have *many* rules about pubs but my main one is this: if there's no natural light going into the pub then neither am I. I've read too much about punishment rooms and the like. Besides, imagine the bent and rickety inhabitants, a cross between Gollum and Mark E Smith, trying to talk to you about football and foreigners, and with a flagrant disregard for the spittoon. No thank you.

This pub was almost the opposite, but awful in a different way. You could see everything through the enormous bulging window. It was lit like your living room and had the vibe of a furnished flat without curtains, or an old people's home without air freshener. I could practically smell the beer farts and hear the crackle of polyester slacks. I could see the patrons milling around inside this great glass bubble. It was like a painting Edward Hopper might have knocked off at his most alienated and depressed.

I tried to ring a cab again. The leatherette protective wallet on my phone was stuck down with melted snow and I eased it away from the screen, wiping it with a damp tissue. I tried the number for the taxi again, but water had got into the phone's workings and every button I pressed just added another five to a dialled-out telephone number. The screen froze under the snowy assault, and I snapped the phone shut, placing it back in my coat pocket.

Snow was building in tiny drifts on the curb side, and snow flew under the red brick of the bridge as I stood stranded on the pavement, fat downy flakes clinging to my coat, my shoes, my hair. I was two miles from home, cold and wet, and would have to walk the entire distance in a gale, without even snowshoes or huskies. And all because I had a beer belly you could rest your pint on. If I had never seen that photo, I would be at home right now in my warm, quiet flat listening to warm, quiet vinyl.

Fucking Neil. Fucking social media. Fucking weather.

And then I let fly, screaming into the white abyss, as the traffic rolled past, content and oblivious:

"Come on then, you shitty, snowy little bastards! I'll have you! I'm *warm*! I'll melt every last one of you! As long as I've got breath in my body, I shall track you down and breathe you out of existence! You want that, do you? Hot breath all up in your grill? Not just breath either—I could fart you into steam—I've got an entire respiratory system here for you, piping hot and waiting for go-time! And don't get me started on my urine! I've got gallons of hot, percolating, caffeinated piss waiting for you! And I won't just be writing my name either—I'll be writing your death warrant! I don't even believe you're all different—you all look the same to me! And that's not racist because you're just *snow*, stupid pointless snow. Go back to fucking Iceland where you came from, you uniform dicks. You're water's backward stepchild. Just fuck the fuck off!"

This went on for some time.

When I eventually got back to the flat, the snow had stopped and it was dark outside. I drew myself a deep, hot bath and sat there, my belly a pale island in the steaming water. I had a DVD somewhere: *Glynis Barber's Anti-Aging Yoga.* Maybe I'd give that a try. Leaving the house to exercise had proved a mistake.

An interesting postscript to this story is that my phone managed to dial a real telephone number, and the stranger I phoned had uploaded the surprisingly clear recording of me berating the weather to YouTube as "Man Screams at Snow". It got respectable numbers too, considering it was just an audio file. American right-wingers adopted it briefly, as I barracked snowflakes, and it fitted their agenda. I became a meme.

Of course, Neil from work recognised my voice. I opened the door to my office one morning and a bucket of polystyrene snow dropped on my head. I heard myself referred to as "Frosty" in the pub on a couple of occasions. Brochures started to appear in the internal mail: "Come and visit Santa and his helpers in Lapland".

Fine.

I Know You're a Seasonal Beast

I HAD A LIE-IN. It lasted until after the Queen's speech. For breakfast I had Bucks Fizz which comprised eight parts supermarket-own-brand cava to one part fruit smoothie. The acid reflux was practically volcanic—I could feel the back of my teeth melting. To combat it, I took some Black Forest Gateau from the fridge. Black Forest Gateau is my all-time favourite hangover food, except for a Sarah Lee strawberry and cream sponge, but they don't seem to make those anymore. Has Sarah Lee gone now? Who is the modern market leader in low-end frozen cream cakes? For the entirety of my life Sarah Lee has been providing a sense of dependable deep-frozen indulgence for any occasion. The cakes were low-cost, cream-heavy hardy perennials, and *so* good in a crisis. But now they'd gone the way of Spangles, Texan bars and Opal Fruits. I know Opal Fruits haven't gone anywhere, but I refuse to call them Starburst. Starburst wasn't meant to make your mouth water. It sounds spiky and arid and hot. It's a ridiculous name for a piece of confectionary.

They are still making Black Forest Gateau, however. Not Sarah Lee, but somebody is, the good burghers of The Black Forest, no doubt. Why "gateau"? Why not "kuchen"? I suppose the Black Forest borders France, so maybe it does make sense: Gateau Sans Frontiers. I wonder what happened in the war. All manner of puppet bakeries springing up over Vichy France, selling a strangely familiar confection named Schwarzwalder Kirschtorte. That must have been hard to swallow for your average occupied Frenchie. Dark days in la Forêt Noire.

I think this one was just made by Co-Op.

Sometimes I'll have a bit of Tiramisu, just to mix it up a bit. But they didn't have any tiramisu. And I prefer Black Forest anyway. Red Velvet Cake was the only other option. It was Christmas, the shop looked like a plague of locusts had performed a trolley dash. But I don't trust the Red Velvet Cake. What is it? Where did it come from? Why is it everywhere? No thanks.

I received two Christmas cards this year, which is two down on last year. I am half as popular as I was a year ago, which is a confirmation of something, I suppose. I did have an inkling but it's nice to see it borne out by the figures.

One of the cards was from Kerry at work, a nice woman who feels sorry for me. The other is from my aunt Silvia, whom I see once or twice a year. She's my only living relative, apart from Roddy, my cousin and her son, whom she doesn't speak to and two others I've never met. I can't remember their names.

I think the name Silvia has something to do with trees and it rather suits her. She's both willowy and tough as teak. She's about five foot tall but has finishing school deportment, so her back is more than straight: her head leans backwards, tipping up at the chin so she can constantly look down her nose at you. She has a spine like a cat's tail. Silvia used to have money, but I think the money's gone now. She lives in a big house full of small rooms and has soft furnishings on her soft furnishings and dust on everything else.

I'm due to visit her this week. Traditionally the visit is on Boxing Day and tradition is a big thing with her, so it will be Boxing Day unless I die of alcohol poisoning first, which I intend to work on.

I open my first bottle of Shiraz.

I haven't spent Christmas with anyone else for ten years. Since mum and dad went, in fact. Ten years on my own in this flat. Ten empty winters, ten half-eaten turkey crowns, the Brussels sprouts mouldering in the salad drawer till February.

Christmas is a time for sharing, so everything in the shops is bloated, multi-packed and family sized. Turkeys are suety balloons, swollen and leaking, the juice running thick with butter. Everything is distended, heightened, louder, too much. Pubs are unbearable, heaving with neophyte drinkers in antlers and Christmas jumpers, staring glassy eyed through the windows of taxis, unable to remember where they live. Public transport is choked, the roads are choked, and the turkey is choked. And you had to have *fun*. You got invited to things. Even I got invited to things. Work do's. But it was never personal, bespoke fun: it was a team-building exercise in enforced jollity, letting your hair down within sanctioned parameters. It's proscribed fun, like being in the Hitler Youth, but with shots instead of shorts. It's both aggressive and immersive and the exact opposite of reaching out to someone. It appropriated you and dictated your behaviour. It told you there's only one way to have a good time and it's not your way.

I turned down the offers this year. I've put up with it for decades, but I just couldn't stand it anymore. I'm no longer at home to the madness of crowds.

Ten years on my own. I inherited the flat. It's mine. I hadn't done much with it—my parents would still recognise it as theirs. I bought a bigger telly. I unpacked my vinyl into the living room. I have a lot of vinyl, and I'm exactly the sort of person who has a lot of vinyl. While the generation before mine destroyed the planet and the generation after smashed avocados and stopped having sex, my generation bought vinyl. Though, in keeping with the times, I've also stopped having sex. I'm accidentally fashionable again.

I may listen to a record later, on headphones so I don't disturb the woman upstairs, though she's probably not there, what with it being Christmas.

What record should I listen to? I own the Phil Spector Christmas album, of course. You still hear it everywhere at Christmas, even though he shot his girlfriend. You never hear Gary Glitter's "Another Rock 'n' Roll Christmas (Another Christmas Rock 'n' Roll)" though, which proves that murdering a woman is preferable to molesting a child in our culture. I don't suppose that's a surprise to most women.

The whole kiddie-fiddling thing was interesting. I grew up, was a child, in the seventies, which is now seen as the Golden Age of child molestation: The Waltham Bop, the sweaty occultism of the Catholic Church, the back-stage-at-the-BBC glory days. You could buy specialist paedophile magazines from news-stands in London. It seems astonishing now, but you could. Everybody had a "funny" uncle, and everybody knew what you meant when you said "funny" . . .

There were comedy child molesters in television programmes, and it was all seen as part of life's rich pageant: some people you met were just predatory boy-hungry child-fuckers. It was a bad thing to be, but it didn't seem any worse than being a "poof"—both would ruin a political career. It wasn't like it is now. Nowadays people want lynching on demand for paedophiles. In our culture desecrating a corpse or bombing an innocent nation in pursuit of its mineral wealth, sorry, *to stop terrorism*, is nothing next to paedophilia.

We used to get locked out of the house when I was a kid, and you weren't allowed back until dinner. You'd walk to school in winter, kneecaps blue-white, thighs dappled purple, unescorted, running the gauntlet of other, rival schools, and it was ordinary.

Nowadays the roads are choked all day by SUVs, a single child buckled into the back of each giant car, a tiny pip in a giant, protective fruit, ripe with new life.

The whole world is about children now. They've colonised the museums, the cinemas—everything must be interactive and educational. And they're all angels, even the nasty ones with bull-terrier eyes pushing over the other kids in the soft-play area. They're perfect angels too.

I still remember my childhood—that's the curse of my generation—we're all still living out our childhoods. And I remember that most children are not angels. They were selfish, nasty, bullying sociopaths. They'd do well on Dragon's Den: as the dragons.

So, Gary Glitter = bad. Phil Spector = Aw, we still like those records, so fuck it. Besides, she got her tits out in a couple of films, so she probably deserved it. Let's listen to "Frosty the Snowman".

They have secret Gary Glitter listening parties now. I read an article about it. Meetings where people get together to listen to the music of the Glam Rock ghoul without fear of reprisal. I expect they must have to vet them quite effectively. You don't want to end up at the wrong sort of Gary Glitter party . . .

Christ, poor sods. They must be worse off than me. Gary Glitter's not all that. Imagine being around at the same time as David Bowie, T Rex and Roxy Music, but twice a year you have clandestine meetings where you spin "Hello! Hello! I'm back again", which is presumably what Gary says at each court-hearing.

I was never molested as a child. I don't feel like I missed out. I was just a late bloomer.

So, what should I listen to? I liked the Christmas Spector record but my go to festive platter is "Christmastime" by the Swingle Singers. The Swingle Singers were a French . . .

. . . oh, her upstairs is in after all. She sounds like she's dragging something across the floor. She's quiet most of the time, we don't even really acknowledge one another in the hallway. But occasionally there are bangs and

crashes and I hear the bottles clink as she goes up the stairs. And, of course, we share the same recycling box . . .

. . . the Swingle Singers were a French vocal group. I think they're still going but the Christmas record is from the 60s. You've heard this music: it's light, jazzy, showily a capella. I love it. It puts me in a Yuletide mood.

What's she doing? Can I hear sobbing? I sit, straining my ears for a few seconds. Her TV comes on. She has a massive sound-bar. It reverberates through the floor, and I can hear dialogue from On Her Majesty's Secret Service. *Good film: the best of the Bonds for my money. I don't like the new Bonds where there are no jokes, and he gets his bollocks beaten with rope through the bottom of a chair.*

She sounds like she's properly getting her Christmas on. Good luck to her. I hope she's okay.

Eventually I opted to listen to Robert Wyatt's *Rock Bottom*, before putting a couple of Kievs in the oven. There's no point in being fancy when you're on your own. And I like Chicken Kievs all year round.

I turned off *Rock Bottom* after "Sea Song" as I realised my mistake. It was something to do with Robert's toothless cockney whine, with the massed banks of subaqueous synthesizers and the words: "Your madness fits in nicely with my own, with my own, your lunacy fits neatly with my own, my very own. We're not alone."

It broke me. I was alone. I was so alone. I had no one to share my lunacy with. I started to cry, and not just muted, snorting, banked down sobbing, but sudden, half-barked wailing. I howled with the ache and the sadness of it all. It rattled my body, and as Robert went for some estuary scat singing—halfway between Pharaoh Sanders and Chas and Dave—I flung the headphones off and sat there on the floor grizzling.

There was a knock at the door, and I wondered how long I'd been crying for and how loud. I could no longer hear *On Her Majesty's Secret Service*. There was another knock on the door. It was a knock that would rather not be there, a knock that would rather not be knocking, a diffident, no-thank-you knock. I froze. I could hear Robert Wyatt's clip-clop percussion through the headphones. There was a rustling sound, and an envelope was pushed under the door. I thought "That's it—it's the woman upstairs. She's giving me a Christmas card. That's all".

The room was suddenly full of noise: angry, bleating noise that hit me like a slap: the Kievs! I rushed into the kitchen to discover the charred chicken breasts aflame. I turned the oven off and waved a copy of *The Fortean Times* at the smoke alarm, until it calmed the fuck down. As I opened the kitchen door, the cold air stung my wet cheeks, and I put the dead Kievs in the bin. I replaced them with two more. I had a freezer full of chicken Kievs.

I returned to the living room and lifted the stylus from the record and, as I picked up the headphones from the floor, I remembered the card sitting by the door. It featured a robin sitting on a Christmas pudding and read: "Happy Christmas to Paul from Julia (upstairs)". It was hand-drawn and quite well done. She must have got my name from my mail.

"Happy Christmas to Paul from Julia (upstairs)".

Julia.

Nice name.

I put it on the mantelpiece with the other two cards, poured another glass of wine and switched on *On Her Majesty's Secret Service*.

Silvia

I LAY STILL in the darkness. I felt I had been the subject of a sophisticated experiment. My eyes were wide and drank in the gloom as I tried to focus on the fuzzy, busy objects that circled my head, like a halo of flies. I breathed in dead leaves and desiccated insects, which settled like dust in a crypt. This was not my beautiful mouth. This was not my beautiful tongue.

I ran the latter over the former. It was dry and smooth: a snake's belly sliding over ruins. What had happened? I shifted my wooden limbs, and something rolled off the bed and fell with a muted clunk onto the carpet. Was it a leg? No, it was a bottle. And then I remembered: it had been Christmas day. And I had been drinking.

I got to my feet and padded to the bathroom and ran my mouth under the cold tap. Life sprang up as though on a dusty alien world, my terraplaned tongue blooming, becoming flexible and exploratory, the roof of my mouth smooth again. I coughed and my voice returned in yaps. I spat into the sink and tannin sediment coloured the saliva like sick blood. I was alive. I felt I had been beaten about the head and neck with a wet rope, but I *was* alive. I resolved to fry an egg in butter and open a can of fat coke. It was the only way I would live through this.

It was Boxing Day. I had survived another Christmas alone, but this was to be a sterner test: Boxing Day in company. It was the day of my annual visit to my aunt Silvia.

Silvia lived in three rooms of a large house on the other side of town. When she was younger, she had red hair and studied ballet, and I think her Sixties had been mildly bohemian—she had been married to an airline pilot, and there were rumours that she entertained gentlemen-callers during his long-haul flights. The family were scandalised: she had become a sort of low rent Princess Margaret in our household mythology. Now I was all that was left of the family, and I wasn't scandalised, I was traumatised: I was going to have to drive across town.

I drank coffee. I brushed my teeth. I vomited. I brushed my teeth again. I dressed and sprayed myself with a *lot* of deodorant. Pressing my head against the cool glass of the front door I stared into the grey glow of the day. Pushing outside I made it as far as the car, applying my hands and cheek against its freezing flanks. I let myself in, dulling the mirror with my breath, starting her up. I made it fifty yards down the road before pulling over and heading back on foot to the house to see if I had closed the front door, which I hadn't. I strolled back to the car, which was shivering in clouds of condensation, the driver's door still open.

As I drove, I let my hands and feet do everything. I did not engage at all. I knew that if my brain blundered into proceedings there would be a major traffic incident. Like those moments of frozen confusion I encountered typing up my notes, where my brain over-took my hands and I no longer knew where the semicolon key was. Besides I was already using my brain to sustain a gentle, fizzing panic. I scanned the landscape for signs of the police, squinting at dark shapes in the cold eye of the rear-view mirror.

I wouldn't have driven ordinarily. I had been asleep and drunk an hour ago and would clearly fail a breathalyser test. But I was late and it was Boxing Day and I imagined the traffic would be quiet and the police, basically human beings, would want to be home with their families. Of course, there were probably policemen like me who had no families and were likely to be vindictive because they were working during the holidays and nobody loved them, so I kept a constant, paranoid surveillance while my hands and feet got on with the job of not actually killing anybody. It worked. I got to Silvia's house ten minutes after I said I would and had not been arrested.

"Christ. You smell like a brewery."

I released Silvia from my embrace. She was brittle and neat, her hair still suspiciously red, her face caked in powder. She wore a baby blue cardigan and pearl earrings and her eyes were fierce in the gypsum mask of her face. She'd left an imprint in dust on the front of my raincoat, like the Veronica.

"I can't believe you drove. You stink like a dosser."

"Thanks very much," I said. "I smell death on you."

"Charming as ever, though you're probably right. I'm properly on my last legs now."

I draped my coat over the end of the banister, and she picked it up with a tut and placed it on the coat-stand and, with a tissue retrieved from her sleeve, attempted to scrub the face powder from my lapel with her spit. I went straight into the kitchen and put on her pinnie and five minutes later I was crushing fennel seeds in a mortar and pestle. She appeared armed with two large tumblers of gin and tonic and two small paper hats.

We'd been doing this every year for the last decade, when I'd got back in touch with Silvia after Mum and Dad's funeral. Our family was always small, but by the time I'd reached my fifties it had dwindled to nothing. Silvia had a son in Australia whom she'd fallen out with, and I had a couple of cousins in America I'd never met. Silvia's husband and my parents were long gone, so this was it. Every Boxing Day I came to her house to cook a chicken which was the only thing apart from steak I cooked well, and then we got drunk in front of the telly together. After dinner the bickering would start and my character would be swiftly atomised and I'd threaten to leave but I never did because she kept a good cellar and my house was miles away, so I took the constructive criticism until she fell asleep with her mouth open, and I fished her loose false-teeth out, so she wouldn't choke and placed them on the coffee table in front of her. Then I would drink quietly on my own, watching the TV with the sound down until I fell asleep. Every year for a decade we did this. I didn't mind. She would never remember the harshness of her criticism. Or would she? There was always faint embarrassment in the morning. She could remember something, but she wasn't ever sure what it was.

I zested a lemon.

"Are you seeing anyone?" said Silvia.

"That question comes earlier every year," I said. "You usually wait until I've finished eating."

"That's a no then?"

"That's a no then."

She prodded me in the belly. "It's cause of this," she said.

"Do you want me to continue cooking you a dinner? I don't have to do this, you know. I could be at home right now nursing a bad hangover."

"I'm not being cruel, Paul. I say it because I love you."

I stopped zesting and looked at her.

"You love me?"

"I have to. You're my last relation."

"You've got a son."

"He's a little shit."

I shook my head. "No Silvia, I'm not seeing anyone."

"I expect you've missed the boat now," she said, sadly. I chopped the garlic.

Dinner was civilized. We drank Pinot Grigio with the bird and listened to a CD of hymns sung by the Kings Singers. The conversation was polite, if a bit dull. Neither of us did much of note and we had few common interests so there were lengthy gaps, which was fine. We knew each other. The silences were comfortable and the chicken was good, so there was no need for chat. The paper hats rustled as we chewed, shivering like butterfly wings over our heads.

After dinner we watched the television. It was an evolved experience, a well-worn rut. Silvia was old and thin and felt the cold, so the heating was blasting. She was slightly deaf, so the TV was blasting, the adverts on the commercial channels punishingly so.

She narrated each programme, often over expository passages which she found boring, so I was briefed on the action that we'd both just been watching, but by the middle of the film we had no idea what was going on.

She had a memory for faces but not names, so every time a new person appeared on screen I was asked "Who is he? I know him." On any occasion that I was able to answer she disagreed with me. "Don't be so stupid. He has a much thinner face." She sat bewildered by the end credits when it was revealed that I was correct, wondering how I'd managed to pull off this feat of legerdemain.

She didn't differentiate between film eras either: every film was happening in one big cinematic now. She was convinced that Joey from *Friends* was in *Arsenic and Old Lace*, despite it being made decades before Matt Le Blanc was born. My favourite question from the evening's viewing was: "Who is that actor who always reminds me of Jack Lemmon?" and when Juliet Stevenson appeared on screen she seemed genuinely angered. I never found out why. "She knows why," was all she gave me.

I was sometimes unable to worry out the name of each actor she was thinking of on demand, though some of the actors didn't appear on screen, their memory being prompted by the appearance of somebody else—it was like playing a game of Guess Who twice removed. She was always disappointed when I couldn't place the mystery person: "You used to be good at this!" she said, as though there were a point in time when I could gaze into her mind and map out her thought processes from no information.

And, of course, she was right; there was a time when I could do exactly that.

I was depressed after the death of my parents and I briefly moved in with Silvia, whom I hadn't seen in years. I'm not sure whose idea it had been, and I soon moved out again as we both quickly realised it had been a mistake. But after a month of intense scrutiny of the box I could accurately map out whole evenings of Silvia's idiosyncratic and active television watching.

Her latest assertion was that Americans couldn't do collars.

"What do you mean Americans can't do collars?"

"Look," she said, as Jimmy Stewart put his foot up in *Rear Window*, "look at his collar. Rubbish."

"He's not meant to look smart. He's a grouchy, down-at-heel photographer with a broken leg!"

"No, they all look bad, all of them. It's the collars. It's just the collars."

I knew what this was. These were the symptoms of loneliness. Silvia was always alone. Watching the television was a bonding opportunity: films were not entertainment in and of themselves, they were springboards to a larger narrative, they were a stepping off point. They *included* me. My aunt knew something I was good at, perhaps the only thing I was good at—naming obscure actors—and wanted me to impress her. When she recapped the start of the story over the middle of the story so ultimately she had no idea what was going on at the end of the story, it didn't matter. That was not the point. I would know what had been happening. I could read a film.

She knew this.

That night she slept upright on the sofa, her head thrown back as though seized with laughter. I removed her glasses. Her teeth had come loose, drawing in and out with each sonorous snore, peeping like a cat's tongue. I removed them and placed them beside her glasses on the coffee table. I fetched a blanket, draped it over her and continued to watch old films on her TV, drinking her wine in silence as I had done every Boxing Day for the past decade. When I finally went to bed, I kissed her on the forehead. In my family we showed affection only when the other person didn't know.

The fight seems to have left her in the last couple of years. She was merely pass-remarkable now, not devastating. There were a few early jabs and then for the rest of the evening she was almost companionable. It worried me. She wasn't herself.

In the morning, as always, she betrayed no hint of the previous night's excesses. She was bright and neat with just the tiniest edge in her manner, as though she was expecting bad news.

"I'm going to go," I said.

"I expect you're busy," she said. She knew I wasn't busy.

"Same time next year?" I said.

"If you like. If I'm still clinging to life."

"You're like lichen on a rock, Silvia. Nothing's going to scrape you off." We hugged, stiffly.

When I got in, I took my jacket off and there once again was the powdery outline of her face pressed onto my lapel. The ghost of a smile.

Nite Flights

I LIKE TO GO FOR WALKS at night, if I'm not too drunk. I like the city after dark: the amber halos around the lampposts, the powdery stone, the restless tide of the traffic. I like the sound of distant drunks, their cries sad as whale-song. I am comforted by the city, held in its arms. These are the nights when I am not haunted by loneliness, nights when I still feel there's some mettle in me. The city at night is softened, all burnished greys, long shadows and dimmer-switch neon. The music of the night is a deep-sea murmur interspersed with sudden crashes of unknown provenance. You keep your wits about you at night, it's hard-wired into you. It isn't fear, it is respect for the dark. The night is wild. It could turn on you without warning.

I love the coolness of the night. The chill of it on my face is a balm after the nervous, excitable days: the hectoring office hubbub, the clammy, impersonal tube, the rawness of crowds. In the night people come in manageable clumps, they're fine if you don't stray too close. You don't want to get sucked in.

My part of town was once a village until it was swallowed by the hungry metropolis and so, beyond the wide Victorian high street, there are row after row of modest thirties semi-detached houses. That's where I like to walk. There's never anybody about. It's mostly young people living round here, younger than me at any rate, people in their thirties and forties. They have little kids so they don't go out. There are lights on in every home.

I'd given up on my novel which was one reason I was out walking. A book about a vampire hypnotist in Belfast: who the fuck wanted to read a book about a vampire hypnotist? And why Belfast? Was there supposed to be a sectarian slant to this? Was the Count going to aid the peace process by proving that once you puncture the skin we're all the same underneath?

I was never going to finish this stupid book and all along I thought the reason was Wainwright, my boring hero, a Sexton Blake manqué with an aquiline nose and a no-nonsense right hook, flapping around Northern Ireland in a trench coat and betraying absolutely no evidence of interacting with the locals. But it wasn't Wainwright at all, it was the Count: Udo Egarhazi, Count Blutwurst, a vampire who drifted into light-entertainment. The big finale was supposed to be Egarhazi at the BBC hypnotising the nation. It would be a dystopian future filled with zombified British nationals waiting to be lazily picked off by the voracious and soulless elite. Like Brexit, you see? Satire.

Wainwright was always going to lose. I wanted a nice '70s "we're all doomed" vibe, and it would set me up neatly for the sequel in which his daughter, Angelica, would exact her explosive revenge with a boot-knife and a white vest top.

But it wouldn't work now. The disintegration of television viewing made my plot untenable: nobody watched TV at the same time anymore. The late '70s was the time. At one point the ITV networks went on strike and the BBC had a complete TV monopoly: *Top of the Pops* got over twenty million viewers.

But people didn't live like that now. They dipped in, they swiped right, they yawned and ignored. A lot of them didn't even bother with tellies. I thought of my flat with its monstrous plasma screen and its books and DVDs and vinyl, the dust forming dunes like desert sand, and I thought of young people with their white-box, Marie Kondo lives, their wireless existences, unencumbered by their shallow pasts or psychometric relationships. Young people attached to nothing. And I wondered why I was trying to write a book for them. A book they would never read, a book that would never be underlined or left, dog-eared and water-damaged on a toilet cistern. *Fuck it*, I thought. Sometimes it really is better not to try. To know when you're beaten.

I decided to go walking in the dark.

I love the softness of the city at night. Its tempo relaxes, its sounds distort. It's like walking on a grey, empty moon. The distance between people lengthens and the people you do see are adrift on a lunar landscape: unbalanced, aware of their own gravity, bobbing like balloons. The air is colder, cleaner, more visible. You breathe it out and suck it back in. It is purifying.

To go out in the day is to be snubbed by strangers, by shopkeepers, neighbours. There is no one to ignore you in the night. It is a safe place, a safe empty space.

Though not for everyone.

Another reason I like to go walking at night, up into the homely terraces that flank the High Street, is to look up at bedroom windows. I want to see a naked woman. I've never once seen one and I've been taking these nocturnal strolls since I was fifteen years old, so that's nearly forty years without a result. That's a kind of madness that goes beyond mere voyeurism. What is it in the male gaze that needs to endlessly violate women? I don't want them to *see* me spying on them. I mean, obviously I don't want it to become a police matter, but equally, that's not the thrill. The thrill is the getting away with it. I want to see them uncovered and unaware, just going about their business thinking they're unobserved. But they aren't— I've seen them, and they haven't seen me.

It's never happened. I've never seen a bared bosom under glass and at this point I don't expect to. But if I did it would be the thrill of a lifetime, a moment of sudden and unintentional bared flesh, the curtains shutting, the blind snapping down, but too late. Other men have loftier ambitions but I know I could die happy stealing a glance at a rogue nipple.

It was slim pickings. As I beetled down the side streets the lights were off and the houses cold, blue and dead. There was an occasional cosy glow behind the closed eye of a shutter. It was a bright night, and I could see stars even beyond the fluorescent fuzz of the streetlights, and it seemed a more pathetic venture than usual under the watch of unending space. As I stared up into pin-pricked infinity, I wondered if there was anyone in the universe more pathetic than I was at that moment: a middle-aged man peeping through bedroom windows hoping for a glimpse of stray flesh. I wasn't even good at it. Forty years and not a shed bra or a carelessly fastened dressing gown, never even the ghost of a pubic bush, nothing. I stood under a lamppost and looked up, beyond the gloomy houses to an empty blackness that went on forever, and there was nothing in it as small as I was. I was worse than nothing. I was a statistically improbable event, nothing squared, just filling in for an abscncc. I was a celestial seat filler, waiting for something more noble to return from the bathroom.

I turned to go home, the weight of the universe on me, staring at the cracks in the pavement and my own heavy feet. Taking a wrong turning I ended up in the flats, a warren of brutalist cement cabins stacked like drunken Jenga. Attempting to get back to the main road I found myself at an unexpected angle to a ground floor flat and staring through a gap in the curtains.

And that's where I saw it.

That's where I saw him.

He was standing in the middle of his living room, the TV remote control in his hand. He was about sixty and naked but for his glasses and slippers. His body was swollen and stippled with grey hair. There were blurry blue-green tattoos on his arms and chest.

His genitals were a neat pink cluster: three eggs in a snowy nest. His foreskin was a toothless mouth, a clown yawning at memories.

Our eyes met in a moment of frozen horror until his face melted into a look of helpless collegiate desperation: "Help me out, mate," he seemed to be saying. "Please leave. I will get over this, but you need to go and let me pick up the pieces of my life. Okay?"

I bolted. I ran to the end of the street. Then I ran to the end of another. I ran until I had to double over, propping myself up on a street sign, nearly sick with the exertion. I knew I would never forget the look on his face. It could have been my face. It probably was my face when I was surprised by the window cleaners. It had taken the violation of an elderly man to cure me of my Peeping Tom addiction—I knew I would never patrol these streets again. Why? What was it that made spying unobserved on notional women an erotic thrill and this experience a disgusting transgression? Was I that far removed from the *idea* of women as people, as opposed to zoo exhibits or ants in an ant farm? Was I really that lacking in empathy? Christ. I should hand myself in at the nearest police station: *I will kill again!*

I didn't go to the police station. I went back to the flat. The woman upstairs was playing music. I couldn't quite place it from the bassline, but it was familiar. I went back out into the hallway and the melody drifted down the stairs and I thought I recognised some of the notes, the vocal occasionally cutting through: "Something, something, make up an ocean, something, something, make up a sea".

It was on the tip of my tongue. I went back into the flat and closed the curtains carefully. I could still hear the bassline: "dum, dum, dum—dum, dum, dum—dum, dum, dum—dum." Was it in waltz-time?

I sat in the dark with my coat on. I needed the dark. I needed the cold. It would disinfect me. It would make me clean again.

"Dum, dum, dum—dum, dum, dum—dum, dum, dum—dum!"

"Tiny Tears" by Tindersticks. The woman upstairs was playing "Tiny Tears" by Tindersticks. How cool was that? It was a song I used to love but hadn't heard in years. The melody washed into my head, the oceanic strings, the lugubrious vocal, the heartbroken lyrics. What a great song. She's up there right now on her own listening to Tindersticks.

I'm not surprised she's single.

Alone and Palely Loitering

I was sorting through some old things. I have boxes and boxes of dusty crap in my flat. Books, CDs, mini-discs, cassettes. I have a lot of shelf space and an inability to throw things out. A lot of men are like this, I think, sentimental about objects. We don't get on with people, but we have long-standing and committed relationships with our *stuff*. There was a point in my life when these objects had use. I'd leave records casually propped up against the stereo to impress people: "Oh, I see you have that Toiling Midgets E.P." "Hmm, oh yes. You could pop it on if you want. It's really rather good." It was an easy shorthand. I knew about music and was therefore a cultured and sophisticated man who was at ease in society and a passionate and adventurous lover. That was the idea at least. In fact, the only people my carefully curated records impressed were other men, men with t-shirts and record bags, beer bellies and Converse, none of whom impressed me as likely Casanovas.

Maybe it was time to throw some of this stuff out. I stood on a chair and lifted a box from the top shelf. The dust was like topsoil, spilling onto my face as I held the box at arm's length. Something slid across the top and hit me between the eyes, something hard with sharp corners. I fell off the chair and the box split in front of me, spilling its guts across the carpet.

I'd been hit by a cassette tape. It was my band's demo, a genuine historical artefact, a postcard from the past. I held it in my hands, light and brittle but, miraculously, except for a faded strip along the edge where sunlight had bleached and frayed the paper, remarkably unchanged. I held the entire recorded output of The Franks in my hand: *The Coterie of Conceits* E.P. (The title had been mine. The rest of the band hated it). It wasn't an E.P. as it was never commercially released, though I noted from the typed inlay that we had two managers, neither of whom I could picture at this distance in time. There were four songs on the cassette, fully a third of all the songs I had ever written: "Hypnothermia", "With the Best Intentions", "But Martha's Rather Harder . . ." and "Oliver's Army" . . .

. . . yeah, about that last one. I was always surprised by the cheerful response I got when I announced the song in concert, and by the near instantaneous murmurs of discontent once we started playing it. I should point out that this was not the Elvis Costello song called *Oliver's Army*. This was a Franks original. I had no older brothers or sisters with albums I could inherit. I had limited resources to waste on records I didn't know. It would have been possible to have made the connection, but I didn't and neither did anyone else in the band except, I later found out, Brendan who *did* have a lot of older brothers and sisters but let me go on singing our "Oliver's Army" because he thought it was funny. The lyric to our song concerned the titular Oliver and his army of girlfriends and was, in fact, based on Brendan. Brendan didn't have girlfriends, but his camp followers were legion.

Twenty minutes of rooting around in the cellar and I located my cassette player. It was a green Wharfedale, sticky from kitchen-grease and slightly melted down one side, having sat next to the hob in my old flat for two years. The CD player didn't work anymore but the cassette player might. I plugged it in, but I wasn't willing to risk the Franks' demo on it untested, and rummaged through a plastic bag full of cassettes, until I found one called *Disco Erotica* which I was willing to submit as a guinea pig. A glitterball of a tune called "Nice and Soft" by a band called Wish started up with no obvious problems, barring the title, so I pressed stop and the cassette slowly levered out, intact, and with a satisfying clunk.

I removed the cassette from the box but, before placing it in the machine, I took out the sleeve to have a closer look. The cover was designed by me, so the band's logo was just Letraset. Brendan imagined he was an expert on graphic design and sneered at my kerning, but he was far too lazy to bother making the cover himself, so it was left up to me. Neither of us would have trusted Stuart and Jason, bass and drums respectively, with our image. It was very much a band of two parts: Brendan and I were the glamorous frontmen, Stuart and Jason the backroom boys: glimmer twins and grimmer twins. In retrospect this seems unduly harsh on Stuart, who was always passable looking and interested in hip hop and Krautrock, exotica that was too bafflingly rich and strange for my narrow tastes. Hip hop was made by scary black people and Krautrock might as well have been from space. I love both now, of course, but in the late eighties the furthest outpost I had reached was The Smiths not putting any guitar *at all* on "A Rush and Push and the Land is Ours". A guitar band with no guitar? *What sorcery was this?*

The Smiths, it is fair to say, cast a long shadow over The Franks. Brendan played a Rickenbacker, and I had a quiff like a loaf of bread. Our songs were called things like "Steve Adores the Stevedores" and "Milk float Misery". The cover of the demo tape was a faded picture of the actress Adrienne Posta, with panda eyes and a kewpie doll pout, pouring salt and vinegar into a bucket of chips. It seemed like the sort of thing that Morrissey would like. And I desperately wanted to like the things Morrissey would like.

The first single I ever owned, bought for my fifth birthday was "Alone Again (Naturally)" by Gilbert O'Sullivan. It was my choice. It came in a paper sleeve and cost fifty pence in new money, which was an amazing sum then. My mum gritted her teeth and bought it for me, presumably thinking it would be destroyed in minutes. She was wrong.

Quite what impressed me about this wistful piano ballad about death and suicide, I don't know. Maybe I liked his hat. Every year, every birthday, I would get a new single. We weren't rich and my parents thought that music was a waste of money. My dad owned two records: Matt Monroe's "Born Free" and "Hoots Mon" by Lord Rockingham's XI. I have no idea why he chose those two records. I wish I'd asked him.

In 1973 I was given Elton John's "Daniel," in 74 it was "Seasons in the Sun" by Terry Jacks. In 1975 it was "S.O.S." by Abba. 1976 brought "No Regrets" by The Walker Brothers and in 1977 it was "Lonely Boy" by Andrew Gold, in many ways the worst of them. "Lonely Boy" was the story of a child who, though briefly happy, gets a sister and is inconsolable. He never gets over this primal betrayal. The galvanising experience of his life was his sister being born. It's an irony that I'm sure was not lost on Andrew Gold that "Lonely Boy" becomes lonely through a surfeit of company.

Even today it's a strange and monomaniacal song. It was by the same man who wrote *The Golden Girls* theme. At the end of the song, the hated sister has a son and he grows up to be a lonely boy too. What is this matrilineal malaise? And why did I like it? I was ten years old when this song came out. And I loved it. I was swept up by its strangeness, those half-glimpsed fragments of story. There was mystery, more than met the eye. Surely having a sister couldn't be the thing that destroyed his life? There had to be more to it than that.

I *was* a lonely boy. I'd spend hours on my own, drawing, reading, listening to my records, all five of them. I knew every note. I knew every kink and skip, every hiss. I knew the lengths of the gaps between songs and how long the outro would take to fade out. I loved all my records. It had taken me half a decade to collect half an album's worth of songs. I began to petition my dad for pocket money and, when I got it, I spent every penny on records, almost all of them in a minor key, almost all of them lovelorn and overlooked.

Morrissey was a button-eyed spider waiting to feast on my adolescent angst. I was sixteen when I first heard The Smiths, and it was appalling timing. The Smiths were to blight my life for the next four years. It was like entering a cult and I would have gladly quaffed the vegan Kool Aid for Morrissey. Like a cheetah on the Serengeti, he only ever went after the weaker ones: the marginalised, the dispossessed, the shut-ins. The lonely boys.

I converted. I grew a quiff. I bought blouses from D. H. Evans. I rummaged Oxfam for dead men's suits. I watched *A Taste of Honey* and *Sleuth* and read *The Picture of Dorian Gray*. I listened to girl groups from the sixties (but not from the seventies and eighties, they were *verboten*). I learned to recognise Avis Bunnage, Victor Maddern and Gert and Daisy when they popped up in the damp Sunday afternoon schedules. I was an apt pupil. And Morrissey gave you the greatest gift of all: freedom from effort. Suddenly, good-looking and popular people were shallow and thick. The herd were idiots who didn't understand you. It was pointless attempting to interact with others because they'd never appreciate or deserve you. How much better to stay in your room and avoid all this abrasive human interaction, how much better to hide away from rough girls with coarse manners and harsh tongues, who were only after one thing. So what if you never had sex, or fun or vitamin D? Morrissey didn't do any of those things and he was the voice of a generation. I wanted to be Morrissey and The Franks was how I was going to go about it. He made me start a band. I was willing to step outside the house for that. I was willing to slum it with Stuart and Jason in a school-hall twice a week, because I was one of the elect. I was going to be a star. The sacrifice would be worth it.

I put the cassette on.

I was never going to be a star.

The surprising thing was the competency. The Franks were alright, no better than thousands of other bands, but not appreciably worse either. The drumming was in time, if slightly rigid. Stuart's bass was fluid and high in the mix. Brendan's guitar was minimal and deft, he knew when to play and when not to play. The bastard was good.

The singing, though. Imagine David Bowie had been in a motoring accident. He'd gone through the windscreen, lost a couple of teeth and passed out. He'd been given a shot of morphine in the ambulance and woken up in a hospital corridor on a gurney, confused and only vaguely aware of the loved ones around him, but desperate to tell them he loved them. That's what the lead singer of The Franks sounded like. Don't think "Well that sounds quite good." It doesn't.

I'd worked very hard on the lyrics, poring over dictionaries, assembling a bricolage of stolen phrases the way Morrissey had taught me, a second generation of cultural affectations. "Hypnothermia" had a bit of dialogue from *Logan's Run*. "With The Best Intentions" cribbed lines from Keats and Larkin. Not that you could understand any of the words. My diction was not the best, and there was a lot of echo on my plaintive whisper. I sounded like Ian McCulloch trapped down a well, realising that Lassie was never coming. The songs were short, heavy on distortion and the choruses tended to be the title sung slightly more emphatically than the verses. Brendan didn't like solos, so there were no solos. "Oliver's Army" had neither chorus nor melody but was a short story I intoned over the music. I can still see the sad faces of the audience as I read it out from a piece of computer paper.

I removed the tape from the machine and put it back in its box, but it was too late: the floodgates were open. I was going to reminisce. I was going the think about those lazy, hazy, crazy days of summer. I was going back to my roots.

It was a summer's evening, and The Franks were playing a gig in a venue called Flix. Flix was barely a bar. I'm not sure what function it originally served, being a white-washed brick tunnel, like a section of unused Victorian sewer that had been repurposed. There was a rudimentary bar halfway down the room and a small stage at the far end. The building looked almost normal from the outside. Inside it was shaped like a thermometer. The bar effectively cut the place in half and there was only room for one person to pass at a time. There were no obvious fire-exits, so if a fire broke out near the stage you were going to die, but it was the eighties, and health and safety was practically advisory.

The walls were adorned with bad paintings of Mickey Mouse and Charlie Chaplin which lent the venue its cinematic name. They were naïve in style like old-fashioned fairground murals and were the only charming thing in the place. We'd played this venue six times and the sound was always bad, the crowd sparse and uninvolved, the walls clammy with sweat. This was The Franks first headline gig by default: the proper band had not shown up and we were asked to stretch our twenty-minute support set to an hour. We decided to play it three times as we didn't know any other songs. There was no dressing room, so we made small talk in a boxed off area at the side of the stage. Our inner sanctum was an outie.

I was 21 and Brendan was 20. We were very thin and very pale, and our hair was very tall and dark. My bedroom stank of Elnett and my mum eventually bought me my own hairdryer as hers was constantly missing. I wore beads and a black blouse open to the waist. I had almost no body hair at this point. I'm not sure when it all started to fill in, like Woolly Willy's iron-filing beard.

Brendan squatted territorially on our rider, a milk crate with twelve bottles of warm Michelob in it. He didn't drink then, but no one was going to steal our beer. That meant four bottles each for the rest of us. Undreamt of riches. We were in our stage clothes which were indistinguishable from our street clothes. My attempts to get the drummer to dress like the rest of us proved futile, but at least he was wearing long trousers and had removed the headband.

A crowd was building, among them our fans. Our fans were, in the main, Brendan's fans. His good looks and ability to strike a pose while playing guitar was a genuine asset on stage, though he did tend to pull focus. As the singer, it was a concern or at least it had been. At the last three or so gigs I had developed a fan-base. Two of them. Sisters.

I forget their names now—this was thirty odd years ago—but I want to say Becky. Everyone seemed to be called Becky then. They were my two fans: Becky A and Becky B. I say they were sisters, they may also have been twins as they seemed to be the same age. They were always together, and you could have taken them for best friends as they looked nothing alike. Becky A was a round-faced redhead with no eyebrows. Becky B was a brunette with a long nose and big ears. Despite those thumbnail descriptions they were both extremely attractive: long and willowy, like a pair of Dracula's brides in floor-length skirts and tank tops that anticipated the '90s by half a decade. They were sisters, possibly twins, and they liked me, not Brendan. It was dizzyingly sexy.

The gig went well considering most of the audience were expecting another band. We gelled convincingly and I was in good voice and, unusually, could hear myself through the monitor. The crowd was cut in two: a small, dedicated throng enjoying being ignored by Brendan, who was playing on his knees and stabbing at his effects pedals with the heel of his palm. In front of me, and I started listing slightly to the right just to underline the point, were the sisters, undulating gently, giggling and drinking a pint of snakebite through two straws.

By the end of the set, I'd screamed myself hoarse and my shirt was clinging to me under the venue's modest lights. Owing to the unusual layout of Flix, we had to come off stage and walk out through the crowd and there were even a few clammy backslaps. The Franks were a hit.

I made my way outside into the cool evening and borrowed a cigarette, which I considered my due for having entertained the crowd for a solid forty-five minutes. I'd expected the rest of the band to follow me but when they didn't, I was quietly pleased. I needed some me time. It'd been our best gig. It was also our longest. We were getting good at this.

I leaned back against the pebble-dashed wall of Flix and stared up at the cool moon, its milk-white back lashed by telephone wires. I exhaled, and blue clouds fogged the firmament.

"Hello Paul."

It was the Beckys. Becky A was holding a beer.

"We thought your throat might be a bit dry after all that screaming." she said.

"You were really good." said Becky B. I took the pint from them, and they beamed at me. They were the same height.

"Thanks." I said. I was being cool to disguise that I was shaking slightly with excitement. "Did you enjoy the show?" I spilled some lager down my chin and gave a lop-sided smile to make it look as if I'd done it on purpose.

"You were really good," said Becky A. "You look good under the lights when you sweat. Sexy." I sweated well. Good to know. They giggled and whispered, and I thought I'd better be charming, though it was going pretty well with me just sweating and dribbling.

"I'm so glad you enjoyed it. You know the band only exists for the fans. We are your creatures."

"We're *your* fans," said Becky B. "We don't really care about the band."

"That guitarist fancies himself," said Becky A. In the '80s "fancying yourself" was the worst thing you could do. I couldn't believe it, not only did they like me, but they actively *disliked* Brendan. I wondered if I should betray him.

"Yeah, he does a bit," I said. And then the cock crowed for the third time.

"His accent. *So* fake."

I grinned. Brendan's accent wasn't fake. He was from a huge Irish family but had been brought up in Manchester. It was another anxiety for me. He seemed far more authentic than I did. He was real, where I was just a soft southerner, even though he was the shandy drinker. The girls thought he was putting it on. It was delicious.

Becky B pulled away slightly, distracted. As she did, her sister moved forward, smiling sweetly under the bar's lights and I could see that she did have eyebrows, they were just very fair, and she pressed her slim body against me and pushed her tongue into my mouth. Cider and cigarettes: the taste of every kiss I'd ever had. So, it was going to be the redhead. Good, she was the one I fancied anyway.

I started to reciprocate, my hands working with clumsy inevitability down her back and towards her bum. She pulled away, slipping out of the light and towards her sister, where they swapped places and suddenly Becky B was grabbing my face and pushing her tongue into my mouth. The same taste: the insides of their heads were indistinguishable. The enormity of the situation became clear. I wouldn't have to choose. I was going to be allowed both sisters. Morrissey was full of shit. This was what rock 'n' roll was all about. Her hand moved to the front of my jeans, and I was making a tentative approach towards her left breast, when there was a disturbance. Her sister was urgently trying to get her attention, but it was too late. A beefy hand was on her shoulder, pulling her away, and then it was at my throat. It belonged to a large, dreadlocked man in a misshapen mohair sweater. He pinned me, gurgling, against the wall, bangles shivering on his arm. He wore a thumb-ring, but I couldn't make out the design as my eyes were filling with tears. My erection disappeared in an instant.

"Fuck sake, Grant," whined the Beckys, "leave him alone. He wasn't doing anything."

"Fucking looked like it, didn't it?" said Grant, in a surprisingly posh voice, "Fucking Morrissey twat."

I was trying to get his hand off my throat, though quietly pleased that he thought I looked like Morrissey even as he was strangling me. He hit me in the stomach with his left hand and I emitted a short, surprised wee. Black jeans in a dim light hid a multitude of sins.

Suddenly he was off me. There was swearing and the sounds of a scuffle. Choking, I fell onto my haunches, eyes streaming, and by the time I looked up Grant was lying on the ground, the bangles up to his elbow as he held a defensive arm out in front of him. There was blood on his lip, and he looked frightened and confused. I hadn't realised how drunk he'd been.

Brendan stood in the stance of a Victorian pugilist, vital under the beer-lights and ready to go again.

"Fuck off out of it," he said. It sounded amazingly tough in his accent.

The Beckys were squatting down either side of the stricken Grant. "She's my girlfriend, man," he said.

"Leave him alone," said Becky 2. Becky 1 cradled Grant's head. I couldn't work out which sister was supposed to be the girlfriend.

"Fuck off out of it," repeated Brendan. They fucked off out of it. There was long tear down the back of Grant's mohair sweater. He had his arms around the waists of both girls as they went. His bangles tinkled like a breeze through tinsel.

"The path of true love ne'er ran smooth," said Brendan, sitting down next to me and offering me a cigarette. He shifted away quickly. "What am I sitting in? Piss?"

"Might be a bit of my pint," I lied. "Thanks."

" 'S'alright," he said, taking a long draw on his cigarette, "I quite like fighting."

"Yeah."

"Not like you, you shit-leg."

"I suppose it must come from having all those brothers and sisters."

"Nah," he said, "I'm just good at it."

We sat outside the venue smoking, my groin damp and cool. It felt like there was blood and dust matting my hair and I was finding it hard to swallow. Brendan squatted on his haunches, his perfect face immobile as he surveyed the passing traffic. His profile could have been carved from marble. He was good at fighting just as he was good at everything. I was beginning to doubt the wisdom of hitching my wagon to his star. I would never shine. I would always be second best, Brendan's plus one. He didn't care. His abilities meant nothing to him. He had no weaknesses. I was Jimmy Olsen to his Superman, Watson to his Holmes, Pie Face to his Dennis the Menace. There was nothing to be done. I was friends with a perfect man. The only thing I could do would be to gradually drift away from him, to slip his orbit and wobble off into the empty reaches of space. Oh, what a lonely boy. But not tonight, tonight I owed him.

"Come on, man. I'll buy you a beer," I said.

"Don't worry about it," he said. "I'm not fussed."

"No really," I said, "I'm getting you a beer. Don't be such a soft cock."

He looked at me doubtfully.

"Alright. I don't suppose one'll hurt."

The Body in the Library

When I have a shower, I dry off in the spare room because that's where I keep my hairdryer. The room is filled with books, books that I have neither thrown away nor read. I buy a lot of books, but I don't read many. Since I made my half century I've just about given up on fiction, my own especially. My novel, *Count Backwards*, the everyday story of a vampire hypnotist and the women who loved him, was not going well. It had entered editing limbo.

What I *should* have done was just write it as a sprawling mass of spelling mistakes, narrative cul de sacs and grammatical grotesques. Never looked at what I was writing. Carried on till it was done. Then I could have reappraised it, had ideas about the shape, what needed to be sharpened or excised. But I didn't do that. About a third of the way through I started to dismantle it, tinkering away, piece by piece, and now it was up on bricks. There was a pool of ink on the garage floor, and suddenly spare bits and pieces, stray sentences and rusted semi-colons, and I knew I'd never work out what they were for or where they were supposed to go. The book had come apart in my hands, the label on a beer bottle as I waited for a date that would never come.

I sat on the floor of my spare-room and started to dry my hair. Around me were hundreds of books, stacked in careless piles, fat and thin, large and small, hardback and paperback, good and bad.

I bought bad books. Supermarket paperbacks from baskets by the till: True Crime or Alien Abduction or the Supernatural. I considered myself the world's leading authority on Gef the talking mongoose from the Isle of Man. There were good books as well: Calvino, Wodehouse, the Russians, a complete set of the Fontana Ghost Book series. *Black Snow* by Bulgakov, *A Dance to the Music of Time* (never read it), and a nice, boxed edition of de Rojas' *The Spanish Bawd* (read a bit of it). *Asterix and the Soothsayer* (Anthea Bell and Derek Hockridge were geniuses). But I wasn't reading any of those books while I dried my hair, cross-legged on the floor. I was reading a book called *In Search of the World's Worst Writers* by Nick Page. It was a list of bad poets, bad novelists and bad playwrights, all of whom were doing rather better in the posterity stakes than I was. They were almost all men, of course, though the title of history's worst writer had been reserved for a woman: Amanda McKittrick Ros. And I wasn't going to have that. I mean it was a bit rich that the worst writer of all time should be a woman. It was typical: out of Western Europe's rollcall of literary ineptitude, the acme of awfulness was a woman, and an Irish woman at that.

No.

Sorry.

Never a traditional prose stylist, McKittrick Ros' writing has many fine qualities. She is ambitious. She is fearless. She is methodical. She cares nothing for niceties or convention or the sanctity of the canon. She ploughs a narrow, distinctive furrow: she is her own creation, a strange flower.

I think I love Amanda McKittrick Ros a bit.

She was sneered at by the tastemakers of the day, and she refused to take it. She wrote them insulting verse. She called them bastards. And when later they feted her ironically, she never fell for it. She never gave an inch. She kept her dignity. I mean, the books are practically unreadable, and I have no idea what she's talking about half the time but, equally, they are singular, monolithic things, full of mad invention and free-flowing unending sentences that challenge meaning, that re-appropriate language. They are labyrinthine screeds of impenetrable, lightless prose, a literary black hole, sucking in ideas and returning nothing, an ominous silence, a trail of ellipses, a semantic void.

I mean, it may not be *good* writing, but how many good writers have that sort of effect? I have stared at paragraphs of her novel *Irene Iddlesleigh* for hours and understood nothing. I could see there were words and I recognised them individually. But she found combinations that rendered them utterly mute, defiant of meaning. The page might as well be blank. Who else can do this? You might call that bad writing. I call it magic.

I continued drying my hair. I'm lucky enough having hair in my fifties. Not too many greys either. My eyebrows have gone mental though. They're long and sharp as fuse wire, strange antennae, picking up peculiar signals. I wonder why this should be as I sit naked on the floor, a damp towel under me. Is there an evolutionary advantage to mad spiky eyebrows, or back hair, or testicles descending year on year, like nervous abseilers?

My body disgusts me now. The grey flesh, the dusting of hair, the reminder of our bestial heritage. We were never meant to live this long. Up until the last century, average life expectancy was something like 38. I'm nearly twenty years post-mortem and it shows. My flesh has the colour and consistency of chewing gum on a warm radiator. It's stringy and grey and hangs low and loose. My body wants to return to the earth, piece by piece. Balls first, followed by belly, tits and chins, all of them pulling away from me, straining to go to ground, my continued existence an inconvenience, a distraction from the inevitability of rotting and feeding, returning my selfishly harvested matter to the infinite. Mother Earth brings all her sons home, clod by clod. We're not made of stars, we're made of dirt and dirt we shall become.

I stare into the full-length mirror in my spare-room. I'm rosy from the heat of the shower and still moist in my hidden and hairy areas: legs, armpits, groin. I've dried my arse with the hairdryer though, propped up on my knees, the dryer on cool, and gently rustling my arse-hairs like a leaf blower. A brown sirocco buffets my balls. They rock gently like recently abandoned swings.

My body is long and lean and pale blue. I'm swollen at the hips and shoulder-less like Tutankhamun. The hair on my back and the sparse scrubland over my chest is greying now and trailing down over the swell of my belly. I notice little twists of flesh at my throat, tiny skin tags. They're new. Another baffling gift of longevity.

I don't mind my arms. They're largely unchanged: veiny and simian but unproblematic, ending in large purple hands, the colour of a cross-country runner's thighs in winter. They're stunted and square, with fat blunt fingers and shovel thumbs. There's no poetry in these hands, no art, nothing beautiful will be shaped by them or touched by them. They could twist a nut or punch a clock, but they could never write a line of verse or cup a breast. They're the dark, livid colour of my cock and balls, and those traitors peek out from beneath my stomach, itself hard and smooth and shiny where there's no hair, a tight ball with a pearlescent sheen. My genitals are internal organs externalised, strange roots dug up from the earth, soil still clinging to the mossy thatch.

Man, the parody of animals. I despair of this ugly collection of objects: the onion-skin limbs, the beetroot extremities, the starchy tuber hub. This clumsy vehicle I'm trapped in. I'm a dalek, its hatred feeding back into it.

I put on my dressing gown.

I start to moisturise my face, attempting to avoid looking at it in the mirror but catching a glance. A pink and grey smudge, the high white ridges of my nose, the raspberry sulk of my mouth. The oyster-coloured hollows of my cheeks. I was stuck with this. Or rather I wasn't—this was my starting point. This was the best it was ever going to be. This was it until it got worse.

I dressed. My toenails needed trimming and my nostril hair was climbing across my face like wisteria up a trellis, but I wasn't ready for detail work. Outside it was a beautiful day and my clothes were proving an effective disguise. No one would suspect the horror lurking beneath. I was cleaned and hidden for another day, ready to take my place in the world, as unreadable, as unknowable as a page by Amanda McKittrick Ros, an utterly remarkable absence. I was barely there.

On the bus I didn't get a second look. I'd fooled them all again and I would keep on fooling them.

I smiled.

BELFAST AND LOOSE

JO HAD BEEN A DANCER. At least that's what she'd always told me. It was hard to imagine what sort of dancer she'd been, as she was five foot two, short legged and had a figure that could only be described as Rubenesque. Obviously Rubenesque wasn't the only way I could describe her, but I'm being polite. She wore it well, though. She had hair like a left bank gamine, all chopped into and messed up. Dressing in all black, she accessorised with amber. She wore huge earrings, huge bangles and a tiny nose stud. It was safe to say that she had the Bohemian thing down. She looked like someone who would be talking earnestly in a New York loft for a Basquiat documentary. If I had a preferred style that would be my style. For women. I don't think I could pull off a bangle or leopard skin Dr Martens.

I'd met her twenty years before when she was temping in the office. I was still there, of course, but she'd done a dozen things since then. She was American, and loud and fun in a way that suggested she'd done a lot of drugs and knew a lot of bands. We'd kept in touch and while that wasn't entirely my doing, it was mostly my doing.

Her current adventure had brought her to Belfast, and I was visiting to do research for my book, some of which was set in Northern Ireland. In a moment of quiet reflection, I would probably have told you the reason I'd set part of the book in Northern Ireland was so I could visit Jo. She was, without doubt, my sexiest friend, and I had been sublimating a volcanic lust for her for two decades. She had an easy self-assurance and a forthright manner that implied she might be terrifyingly greedy in bed. And she always smelled so good. It was something heavy, oily, a smoky musk. I could smell it on myself for days after I'd met her though we rarely touched. She was all curves and elegance like something carved from marble. She glided into rooms. She had grace. I'd been in love with her for twenty years and she was too clever not to realise. Nevertheless, she liked me. I could be witty with her. She made me up my game.

Before I got on the plane for a weekend's research into the ins and outs of Belfast (it's not a big place, I reasoned—a weekend would probably cover it) I collected my best clothes, pressing them neatly and packing them with care, in a futile attempt to impress her. I was modish and neat with my button-down collars, tight jeans and polished, heavy soled brogues. She'd called me "preppy" once and it dictated the way I'd dressed ever since. That might sound pathetic, and I can see it is, but compliments have such rarity value in my life that I can't help acting on them. I'm not even sure it was a compliment, but I've dressed like someone who listens to acid jazz ever since. And that was a stupid thing to do if I was trying to impress her: Jo liked giant men with beards and tattoos, men who looked like they might be able to raise a barn or fashion a small boat from a single piece of wood. Jo's husband, Paddy, had a lustrous Victorian cricketer's beard, but also the misfortune to work in I.T. He was from Belfast, and they'd moved there so that he could be near to his ageing parents. He now spent all his time with them as, within six months of arriving in Belfast, Jo had taken up with a hirsute guitarist named Joe Allen. I'd assumed that was his full name, but it was just his first name.

As Jo's friend I was expected to take her side in this, but I'd met Paddy and liked him, he was a sweet man once you got past the accent, and she'd dumped him for the sort of bloke Hadrian's Wall had been designed to keep out. Still, I didn't tell her this, and reassured her she had every right to be free and happy, and the little sociopath ate it up.

Jo met me at George Best City Airport. I'm not making that up. That's what it's called. The airport is about the same size as the average car dealership, so it was hard to miss her, especially as she was holding up a sign with my name on it, because she was hilarious. She gave me a hug, crushing the cardboard sign, and imprinting me with her scent for the next three days.

"Reverb," she said, "so good to see you, little man. What you wanna do first? The murals and shit?"

I had no interest in seeing the murals, but she took me to look at some murals at the bottom of the Newtownards Road anyway. There were men in balaclavas, there were red fists, and there was a lot of passive aggressive stuff about everybody picking on loyalists. What was more discomfiting were the smaller details. The caged windows on a nearby estate and the fortress-like church on the corner of the Short Strand. The constant tongue-clicking of the red, white and blue bunting on the power lines.

I wasn't keen, so we walked into town under rusting bridges, past tattered billboards and scrubland, crossing a bridge and into the city centre, Jo two steps ahead of me, chattering away. I was carrying my weekend bag and anticipating sniper fire.

We arrived at Belfast's Cathedral Quarter and from this point everything was a pub or a restaurant. In what amounted to little more than what Americans would call a city block, I counted fifteen restaurants and thirteen pubs and bars, plus a tiny shop with a smiling man in a pullover outside that exclusively sold Irish Whiskey. This was Jo's favourite part of the city, and it was easy to see why. Non-sectarian murals loomed out at you from every surface. Brobdingnagian duellists had a go at one another in front of a dead dog on the wall of The Black Box, but once you turned left into Commercial Court it went into hyper drive. There was stuff on every surface. The alley was tram-lined with red benches and the sky overhead was a cat's cradle of red lightbulbs and blinking umbrellas. Pub signs were nailed to everything, the cobbles littered with fire buckets studded with spent cigarettes; above them dusty crimson flowers hung in forgotten baskets. Tucked around the corner was a nightmare vision of naïve painting and semi-local celebrities. Here you could see Gloria Hunniford leering up between Van Morrison's legs should you wish to do so.

We repaired to the John Hewitt. The John Hewitt is a proper pub. There are tables that give you sticky elbows, uninspiring wine choices and the faint smell of bleach. All is dark wood and gloom. My kind of pub then. The only concessions to modernity are a couple of pumps of craft beer and a wall dedicated to exhibitions of local art, art which suggested The Troubles were still affecting people in strange and horrifying ways.

Sitting with my back to the wall and with a pint and Jo in front of me, I finally began to relax. Or relax as much as I could in Jo's company. There's an exquisite pain in spending time with a woman you are incredibly attracted to and who has no interest in you at all. It's torment, and yet I still wanted to wring every second out of it, because it's just so rare. An attractive woman choosing to spend time with me, enjoying my company. I drank in the scene with the intensity of a series of SLR photographs, my brain barely coping with the synesthetic saturation: there was a slight shine on her nose, the small pin there glinting under the pub lights. The glare of the whiteness of her breasts plunging into shadow, the pale bites of chipped nail varnish as her short fingers curled round a pint pot. Kohl flicks at the corners of her eyes disappeared into creases as she laughed at her own jokes. It was so dizzying that I frequently lost track of the conversation and was forced to back-track or just grin stupidly.

"Sharpen up, Reverb," she said.

"What?"

"I'm being hilarious. I need an appreciative audience."

"Sorry," I said, "I'm just so dazzled by your beauty I can't concentrate. It'll wear off as the afternoon wears on."

I smeared this with a thick impasto of irony, masking how close to the truth it was. She wasn't buying it.

"What happened to you, Paul?"

"What do you mean?" I said, worried she'd clocked me staring at her cleavage once too often.

"You seem sort of sad. Like, defeated . . ."

"Well, you don't beat about the bush, do you?"

"C'mon Paul, we've known each other too long to dick around. What's ailing you, boy? Spit it out. You seem lost."

This seemed both unduly harsh and deadly accurate and I was stung. I'd got on a plane for this.

"I don't know what you mean." My arms folded themselves on top of my belly.

"I think you should get a girlfriend. You're on your own too much. You've crawled into yourself. You're like a worm in a bottle of tequila."

"I don't think that metaphor really works," I said, "worms don't crawl into the bottle by themselves."

She gave me a big-eyed look.

"You do."

"I would love a girlfriend," I said, "The charms of bachelorhood are increasingly discreet."

Jo looked at me thoughtfully.

"I'm going to make you my project," she said.

"Don't make me your project."

"No, I am. I've thought about it and I am."

"I'm asking you nicely. Do *not* make me your project."

She looked put out.

"Why are you refusing to be my project? I want to put my incredible array of gifts at your disposal."

"I bet you do."

"It's the height of perversity that you don't want me to deploy my particular set of skills to get you laid. No, I'm doing it whether you want me to or not."

"Look," I said, "do not do this thing. No good can come of it. Have you any idea how emasculating it is to be worked on? I'm not a bird with a broken wing, I'm a solvent, experienced, well turned-out middle-aged man with all my own hair. I should be beating them off with a shitty stick."

Jo looked about theatrically for the non-existent, shit-beaten women. I anticipated this move however and used this distraction to get a good look at her tits. So, who was the real winner there?

"I think you need an intervention, Reverb, a timely one."

"I'm begging you, Jo. Please no."

She relented, her hands raised in surrender, and we spent the rest of the afternoon in fond reminiscence and moderately heavy drinking, until a traditional Irish band started a session, and we went round the corner to The Black Box, where a man in glasses was playing African electro from a laptop at conversation crushing volume. We got a cab back to Jo's where she opened the red wine and got the vinyl out, and I fell asleep on the sofa. It was the best evening I'd had in years. Since the last time I'd seen Jo, in fact. Seconds before drifting off I looked up at her, swaying, eyes closed to "Torch" by Soft Cell, and I thought this is what it's like, being in a relationship with someone you like.

Amazing.

And I fell asleep with a smile on my face, dreaming of nothing.

I woke up with a delirious hangover and an unshakable erection.

"Good morning, sunshine," said Jo, breezing into the room and heading for the kettle in the kitchen.

"Coffee?"

"I'd prefer tea, if you have it." My voice had rusted in my throat.

Jo was wearing the remains of yesterday's makeup and a black kimono. That appeared to be all she was wearing. I wondered if she owned any clothes that weren't black. The proximity to her barely covered body, the intimacy of her matter-of-fact manner—she was just going about her morning, unselfconsciously and naturally—was incredibly arousing. People pay for this sort of thing, the girlfriend experience. It made even the fact we hadn't had sex seem authentic. She bustled into the room and, after deciding the cup was too hot to hand over, placed it on the floor in front of me. The kimono slipped slightly and, almost by accident, I caught a glimpse of her nipple. Her hand snaked to the gown's opening instinctively, but it was too late, and my cock suffered agonies of confinement. I bent forward as she righted herself and swept off back into the kitchen.

"Do you want any breakfast?" she said. "Only I haven't got much in. I meant to go to the shop but . . ."

"I'm happy with my tea," I said, but all I could think about was the nipple, as my penis dug into the waistband of my jeans. She came into the room and perched on the arm of the sofa, exposing a length of white thigh. There was a tattoo on her calf I hadn't seen before, a yin and yang. Bit pedestrian, I thought.

"We should get an Ulster Fry. They don't stop banging on about Ulster Fries here. It's the national dish."

"That's new," I said, indicating the tattoo. She flexed her leg casually giving me a better view of her calf.

"Oh, that. Yeah, I don't know what I was thinking. I forget it's there." She stretched like a cat, and I decided that was enough.

"I think I need to use your bathroom."

"You don't need to ask."

I hooked the handle of my weekend bag with my toe and dragged it slowly towards me, inch by inch, until it was near enough to reach down and pick up. I rifled through it and extracted my washbag and, with the washbag covering my groin, rose gingerly to my feet and began a hobbled journey to the bathroom, a towel draped over my forearm like a maître d, and all under the watchful eye of Jo. She said nothing. In the bathroom I locked the door, turned on the taps and popped the button at my waistband, finally releasing my penis, which was furious and red, like a man arguing with a deckchair attendant. It was hard as wood and had fabric patterns bitten into it by the elastic, but at last it was free. The chill air of the bathroom was a cooling balm as it continued to strain like a dog on a string. I ran it under the cold tap. It was glorious but I knew it wouldn't be enough, so I set about the serious business of wanking. It felt discourteous masturbating in someone else's house, but I knew I would have no respite until I'd gotten it out of my system. And besides it was hardly my fault, she was the one parading around in the semi-nip, flashing her breasts and thighs, what did she expect? I was just a man, despite her concerted efforts to ignore that fact.

It was a straightforward operation, and I reached a powerful conclusion in a couple of minutes, well within the acceptable parameters for taking a dump. I flushed the toilet—the prestige moment of my illusion—and sloped back into the living room to my waiting cup of tea, a serene smile on my face.

"Is it safe?" said Jo.

"It's fine," I said.

"Okay, I'm just going to grab a quick shower."

I no longer cared. The thought of Jo in the shower, water running over her naked body, had no further hold over me. I was cured all right. I'd clearly done the right thing, I thought to myself, as I picked up the tea and took a sip. It had cooled to a pleasantly drinkable temperature.

"Paul?" Jo's voice called out from the bathroom.

"Yeah?" I said.

"Why is there semen on my bathroom mirror?"

Long Weekend

Jo and I agreed to go to the Ulster Museum. There was a Gerard Dillon exhibition on that I wanted to see, and it was something that we could do together in Belfast that wasn't drinking. I was hoping to hold off going to the pub for as long as possible, because I realised that Jo saw me as some sort of enabler. I was surprised that her boyfriend, the troglodyte troubadour Joe Allen, wasn't in evidence. "He's off on tour," she said, vaguely. I harboured muted fantasies about seducing her in his absence, but probably no more than any other woman I talked to for more than two minutes. Besides, we both knew that any romantic relationship we might have had would have been twenty years ago, and while Jo was still a very attractive woman, I was very much on the slide. I'd let myself go so far I was experiencing closure.

When we arrived at the museum somebody was waiting for us. It was a woman. She had glasses, red hair and an enormous scarf, and as soon as I saw her, I knew, I knew despite her protestations, I was still Jo's project. And so was this poor woman.

"You fucking arsehole!" I said under my breath as we climbed the steps outside the museum.

"What?" she said. She didn't even have the decency to feign innocence. She smirked.

"Paul, meet Maura. Maura meet Paul." We shook hands and she smiled, and I racked my brains for something to say.

"Hello, Paul," she said.

Genius. Why didn't I think of that?

"Hello, Maura. Hope I'm going to see a lot 'Maura' you over the weekend."

It hung in the air like a leaf on an updraft, a really embarrassing and shit leaf that no one would ever press between the pages of a book and keep forever as it was dreadful, and everyone hated it.

After a short eternity, Jo said, "Didn't know you had kids, Paul."

"I don't have kids," I said, flustered by the non-sequitur, "you know I don't have kids."

"But that's the finest example of a 'dad joke' I've ever heard. You're wasted—you should be driving your mortified teenage daughter to her school formal." They both laughed at this, Maura even more so than Jo, especially when I countered with "What's a school formal?"

Fine.

That's the way it was going to be. I was a figure of fun. It set the pattern for the rest of the day. Maura and Jo kept the laughter flowing by mocking everything I said, laughing at my clothes, my accent and my interests. Jo had known me forever and had an encyclopaedic knowledge of the harmless things I enjoyed: the records, the films, the games. They ruined the exhibition for me, sniggering like schoolgirls when the gallery attendant told them off for their disrespectful behaviour. It was galling.

By the end of the afternoon not only did I not fancy Maura but was distinctly cooling on Jo. She'd laughed down twenty years of infatuation. I had the feeling, rather too late, that I'd wasted decades of unreciprocated lust on the wrong woman, like that bloke out of Proust, and I was positively gasping for a drink. I imagined sitting down for a pint might sort them out but, if anything, it made them worse. And yet I still played along, peppering the conversation with wit and wisdom gleaned from thirty years of pub quizzes. They laughed at the wrong bits, talked over the punchlines and spent fifteen minutes in the toilet together, while I sat on my own, flipping beermats off the top of my pint like my mate Brendan did. I could see, finally, why he did it. He was bored out of his mind.

Jo came back from the toilet alone. My arms were folded in front of me, resting on my belly again. I no longer cared. I'd relaxed the stomach.

"Where's Maura the borer?" I asked.

"Ssh!" she said.

"What do you mean, 'Ssh!'?" I said, "I haven't got a word in edgewise all day!"

"Ssh!" said Jo, "she's at the bar. Be quiet. She likes you."

"What do you mean 'She likes me'? She's spent the day laughing in my face. We're not in nursery school."

"It's just her way, Paul. She likes the craic."

And there it was: the craic. I'd finally encountered the craic. On holiday on the island of Ireland it was impossible to avoid the craic, even if you were English, traditionally the mortal enemy of craic. We were a nation of polyfillas. But why did the craic have to be here and why now?

"What the hell does that mean?" I said.

"The craic. It just means having a bit of a laugh."

"I know what it means. Believe me, I've had some craic in my time. I've had more craic than Whitney Houston!" Jo looked appalled.

"Paul. I must say that's in very poor taste . . ."

"Well, c'mon, you know . . ."

"She *died*, Paul."

"Yes, I'm sorry. And that poor child . . ."

"I'm fucking with you," she crowed. "Christ Paul, when did you become so easy? She likes you. She thinks you're nice."

"How do you know?"

"A woman knows."

"I'm not a woman. What are the tell-tale signs?"

She rolled her eyes. "I don't need signs, Paul. She told me in the toilets."

"What did she say? Use the exact words."

"No."

"Oh."

"It was 'He's quite nice' or something."

That qualification had the ring of truth about it.

"Well, I don't like her," I said.

"Oh, what do you have to do with it? You're a man."

It was hard to argue with that logic. I was a man, and my feelings wouldn't come into it. I was lucky to even have feelings. Then it struck me—I might get to have sex, sex on holiday, like a normal person. Like a holiday rep in Magaluf, methodically grinding his way through a hen party for the ITV2 cameras. And, alright, the sex wouldn't be with Jo, but it *was* with a woman, and Maura wasn't too bad if you really looked at her. She had a round, pretty face, freckles, lively brown eyes. I hoped she shaved her legs. This was a bit hypocritical of me as I was an enthusiastic fan of a hairy vagina and even hairy armpits, which I thought sexy after a Bohemian manner, redolent of sulking, smoking and long French nipples. But hairy legs, no. That's a fur too far. Like being in bed with a prop forward. Still the potential was suddenly exciting and, frankly, I was no prize either. Lanky, grizzled and with an eight-months-gone belly lowering over my genitals like a disappointing sunset. I wondered if I could keep my shirt on throughout the transaction, but the only things I could come up with were medical conditions, weeping sores or allergies. What about a bad tattoo? A swastika or Gary Barlow's face? No, that would never work. If someone told you they had a bad tattoo you would *demand* to see it. I'd just keep the lights off. I'm not that bothered about seeing her naked either. I'm sure she'd *feel* nice.

While I was lost in these thoughts, Maura returned from the bar with pints of Guinness for the girls and a pint of Yardsman for me. The men of Northern Ireland drink Harp or Coors Light, but even I don't hate myself that much. There's a very high suicide rate here.

I reappraised Maura. She was very pretty in a scrubbed clean, out-doors sort of way and her breasts were excellent.

They were both still gabbing away, so I found a flattering angle under the beer-light and tried to make eye contact with Maura. I set my stare to stun.

"You alright, Reverb?" said Jo. "You look like you're sitting on a fart."

More uproarious laughter.

"Maura," I said, "I feel like we haven't really had a proper conversation all day. Jo's yapping has rather eaten into the chat."

"You know women," said Jo, drily, "Gassing on. We can't help ourselves."

I ignored her. "What have you two been talking about?"

"Jo was just telling me that you spunked over her mirror this morning."

I knew that I would never have sex with this woman. Indeed, it seemed unlikely that I would ever have sex with anyone ever again. My life as a sexual entity was now defunct. I was post-sexual. All that energy would have to be funnelled into some other project: collecting imported Japanese vinyl perhaps or making famous monuments from matchsticks. Home-brew, sudokus or serial killing. The shed-bound busy-work of the sexually displaced older gentleman. It was liberating, like sloughing off a tight and restricting skin. The relief. I would be reborn a lissom neuter, blithe and weightless with near endless free time. Finally at peace.

"She said there was a surprising amount," said Maura.

"What really impressed was the height," said Jo, "not bad for a man in his fifties. Some of it was eye level!"

"Ouch," said Maura.

I drained my pint and went back to the bar.

That night I lay on Jo's sofa. I was very, very drunk. At some point Maura left, and Jo and I went back to the flat. The evening was a virtual repeat of the previous one: red wine, Guinness, records strewn around the room, Jo dancing on her own in the middle of the rug, lost in music. The difference was I was now sulking. I hadn't managed to break my mood from earlier and, at one point, when I'd refused to dance with her for the seventh time, Jo and I had a nasty argument, a barked and bitter airing of grievances. She swept grandly out of the room and slammed the door. I spent twenty minutes drunkenly trying to turn her stereo off and was now lying on my back looking at her ceiling. Coving. You didn't see so much of that nowadays. Creamy and smooth. Beautiful.

I'd made no notes for my book, which was why I was supposed to be in Belfast, because I had been drunk for forty-eight hours. The city had been a blur of murals, strange public art, checked shirts and those weird party buses where you had to pedal and drink while someone plays The Venga Boys. The streets were full of them, clogging arterial roads, delighting no one. The whole weekend had been a farce from start to finish and the biggest farce was that I didn't give a shit about the book. I'd all but given up on the thing. The reason I was here was to spend time with my sexiest friend, and that had been shameful. About halfway through the evening I'd concluded I didn't much like Jo. She was selfish, she was an attention seeker, she had very little empathy and fewer social skills, especially when she was drunk, which was all the time. What was worse was I still fancied her. I probably fancied her more for meting out this miserable treatment. Even now, lying on the sofa, drunk and furious, I was thinking about her: her black hair, the rolling abundance of her flesh, her huge black eyes. God. I pulled the blanket over my face and begged the cosmos to put me out of my misery. Either unconsciousness or death would have been fine.

The door creaked. I could hear scuffling and a sort of wheezing breathlessness. I pulled the blanket down. Jo was on her hands and knees crawling towards me, sniggering. I was surprised to see she had drawn whiskers and a black triangle on her nose. The noise was supposed to be purring, I think.

"I'm a cat," she said.

"Right."

"Aren't you going to ask 'miaow'?" she said, adding. " 'Miaow'. Like a cat would say."

"Right."

I was primed for further ridicule. I didn't know where this was going. She seemed drunker than she'd been when she'd gone to bed, so anything could happen. I was expecting the worst. When she reached me, she started rubbing her head against my chest and making her purring noise, which sounded like a horse choking. After a few minutes she stopped and looked at me.

"What's the matter? Don't you fucking like cats?"

She had red wine stains around her lips and her eye makeup had detached and made a bid for freedom. Her eyes, still beautiful, were having trouble focusing and her voice was thick. She gave a lopsided smile as though she could no longer negotiate both sets of cheek muscles. Her kimono had come undone, and I tried to focus very hard on her eyes which made it even more difficult for her to look at me. She frowned.

"I'm preparing myself to forgive yourself," she said.

"Thank you."

"You may make love to me, if you want. I know you want to."

I levered myself off the sofa.

"You're a very beautiful woman, Jo," I said.

"I know, I know," she said. "Take me to bed or lose me forever."

I put my hands under her arms and lifted her to her feet.

"Time for bed," I said. She frowned at me again, her eyes drifting.

"Will *you* take me to bed?"

"Of course."

"Thank you."

I walked her to her room. She fell on the bed, and I pulled a blanket over her. She had closed her eyes and was starting to murmur.

"I always like you, Paul," she said.

"And you, Jo. Get some sleep. See you in the morning."

I turned out the light and walked back into the lounge. Lying down on the sofa, the blanket over my face, I waited for death to take me.

The Babysitter

When I got back from the airport Brendan was asleep on my doorstep. There was a half-finished bottle of J P Chenet in his hand and there were white scuff marks on his knuckles. It looked as though he had attempted to steady himself by punching the brickwork. I looked about. My street was usually quiet despite being off the high-street, but I expected that at least one of the neighbours would have seen him, and social media would be alive with twittering and curtain twitching. Some of the younger denizens of my street had started a WhatsApp group, which I declined to join as it was mostly posts about parking and schools, neither of which interested me. But a tramp expiring on my doorstep? That was proper goss. I could sense the chatter all about me like insects busy on a summer's day.

I nudged Brendan with my toe. There was no response—maybe he was dead. He looked awful. His skin was grey, his lips stained and chapped. His knees were drawn up against his chest, his left foot falling at an awkward angle from the doorstep. The doorstep was wet, and I had to wrack my brains as to whether it had rained today. I recalled, with relief, it had. Brendan looked like a body cut from a peatbog: the straggling beard, the foetal contraction, the obvious signs of violence, though in this case it was likely self-harm. I kicked him again, hard and meaning it. He came to with a snort, and sent the bottle flying.

"What is it?" he said.

"Brendan," I said.

"Paul." He looked around with one eye. His voice was parched and cracked. "You owe me a bottle of wine."

I pulled him up by the arm and he braced himself in the doorway. Unlocking the door I pushed him inside. Over the road I could see one of the neighbours, a young woman in corduroy dungarees, filming me on her tablet. I flicked her the Vs and went inside.

"I'm not joking," Brendan said, "have you got anything to drink?"

"What the fuck are you doing, mate?"

He shot me his most charming smile. I was not charmed.

Five minutes later Brendan was lying on my sofa sipping daintily on a glass of Shiraz. I'd made him take his boots off, and then made him put them back on again once I'd seen the state of his socks.

"What do you mean, Paul?" he said. His voice had returned to normal: low, sibilant and vaguely mocking. He believed he had the measure of the situation. He was lying in comfort on someone else's sofa, drinking their wine. In his scheme of things this was a positive outcome.

"You're in a bad way, mate. You must see that. I get in from the airport and you're asleep on my doorstep clutching a bottle of wine. That doesn't look too clever."

"I was waiting for you, you melt. I was visiting you. What's wrong with that?"

"You were unconscious."

"I was tired. I had a little sleep. I don't know why you're being so aggressive—this is a perfectly normal social interaction."

With effort he propped himself up on one elbow and poured some more wine. His white quiff was longer and greasier than usual, and I noticed a bald spot, the skin freckled at his grey crown. He threw his head back with the reflex-speed of someone hiding sudden nudity. I found myself looking away, sparing him. He was relaxing. His feet kicked up on and down on the arm of the sofa. He didn't seem to notice the business of his feet. His extremities were a constant blur.

When Brendan and I were young we were wary of one another. He was Northern, which was exotic. He was supposed to be clever. He was said to have immaculate music taste. He was the boy all the girls fancied. All these things were quite easy to believe, especially the last one. I wasn't quite ready to believe that anyone had better music taste than me, but even I had to admit he was a bit of a looker. Brendan was blessed with dark wavy hair, gypsum skin and huge blue/green eyes, framed by long dark lashes. It was the kind of beauty that could break into bank vaults, a face that could get him into any room and out of any situation. I wondered whether that was what was destroying him, this unasked-for gift, the power to do anything, and the loss of that power through the simple fact of his continued existence. The longer he lived the further he got from his golden youth, when he could have done anything and chose to do nothing. Brendan had squandered his gift. He'd had sex with neither boys nor girls. He hadn't excelled in his studies. He barely showed up for classes. His teachers, all in love with him, begged him to do the bare-minimum, but he refused with a smile. He stayed in his room, smoking and listening to records.

I got to know him at gigs. He would appear wearing terrible clothes, in which he somehow looked glamorous and important. He was surrounded by girls and boys who bought him drinks all night and whom he ignored. I decided I needed to know him. Brendan was witty, disparaging, and supremely confident in his opinions, of which he had many. There was also, and this might be hindsight, but I think it was there even then, a terrible anger in him, as though he were the victim of some nameless injustice. It was barely banked down and would rise like venom during his more poisonous attacks on friends. All of Brendan's worst brickbats were reserved for his friends, and I was glad no one ever reported back what he said about me.

When we started the band, as a way of becoming friends, I was very aware of being a singer in a band who wasn't as good looking as the guitarist. It was as if we had broken some natural law, and the audience never forgave us. I could never stage-dive as the crowd always drifted stage-right to where Brendan was playing. I usually sang to a semi-circle of floorboard. We weren't a stage-diving band anyway. The Franks ambition was to be The Smiths. Not the next Smiths, the *actual* Smiths. But The Franks sounded like The Cure at their spindliest, with Scott Walker on vocals, if Scott had his tongue wrapped in bandages. We did a few gigs, we made a demo tape, we had a bit of interest from a local label, and we started drinking heavily. Eventually the gigs stopped happening, the interest petered out and the band broke up. But we carried on drinking.

And here we were. Brendan was drifting off again, but I was angry with him and wouldn't let him sleep.

"You can't go on like this," I said.

"You're the one going on," he murmured.

"Mate, you look like a tramp, you stink like shit and you're falling down pissed in the street. You carry on like this, you're going to die."

"I don't mind," he said.

"Well, I fucking do! Don't do it on my doorstep!"

He opened his eyes. "And there you have it. 'Go ahead and kill yourself, Brendy, but do it where I can't see it.'"

"I don't want you to die. I just don't know why you're doing this to yourself."

"Doing what to myself?"

"The drinking. All the drinking, all the time."

Brendan buried his head under the arm of the sofa.

"You're not exactly spearheading a temperance revival yourself, Tubs," he said.

I let it go.

"I just don't understand you, this. You had it all . . ."

He rose and suddenly and there was the anger. His face was white and his words sharp.

"What did I have? What exactly did I have, Paul?"

"I dunno. You were cool."

"You fucking child," he spat, " 'Cool'. Grow up you simpleton. I suppose *you're* still cool with your t-shirts and your cosy vinyl and sitting on your arse in your dead mum's flat, chasing down hot new bands who are thirty years younger than you. They don't want you at their gigs, Paul, you fat clown. You're an embarrassment to them. You look like their dad. But you've heard of them, Paul, you've heard of them and that's what matters and that's what makes you so fucking cool, isn't it? Straight from the fridge, Daddio."

"Get out," I said.

"You what?"

"Get out of my flat." I said it and I meant it.

"Now, Paul . . . mate . . ."

I stood over him, shaking with rage. He was shrinking with his bald spot and scuffed glasses, his missing tooth and incidental beard. I looked at the worn instep of his ruined boots, the button missing from his shirt, the frayed turn-ups on his jeans, the busted fly yawning at me. How had he let this happen? As empty and worthless as my life was, as devoid of human kindness, of softness, as paunchy and bedraggled as I had become, I was better off than Brendan. Because even though every one of his problems was his own doing, his inability to adapt, to accept changing circumstances, to listen or learn, he always *knew* he was right. He never had a moment's doubt. There'd been a mix up somewhere, some cosmic human-error that would eventually be cleared up, revealing Brendan, the master logician, alone in unfailingly getting it right every time. I began to realise that my self-doubt, my mistrust of myself, was a form of self-defence. If I was always wrong, I would never have to be right. I could be guided, moulded, taught. I could learn things. I could improve. And I remembered back to when I was a teenager and unable to show weakness, unable to fail and consequently unable to do anything at all other than back-comb my hair. Life had beaten all of that out of me, life had tenderised me. I was workable.

Brendy was a flawed diamond, utterly himself and unable to change. He was an alcoholic tramp who'd never made a bad decision in his life. Every one of his good choices had led to this.

"You're not going to chuck me out are you, pal?" he said. "I came to see you."

I went into the kitchen and came back with another bottle of wine.

Later in the evening Brendan told me a story. I've changed it slightly for coherence and brevity.

"I went to rehab, you know, to dry out."

"What?" I said, "When was this?"

"About six months ago. The ex sorted it." He spat the word "ex". I'd never heard him use her name since they'd split up. She was always just "the ex".

"That was . . . nice of her," I said.

"Her new bloke sorted it. He's got something to do with . . . medicine or something. Anyway, he paid, so I thought 'fuck it.'"

"Your wife's new boyfriend paid for you to dry out?"

"Yeah," said Brendan, as though that was the least that he could do. "So, I went in, and you know what? It wasn't that bad. I mean, there were some boring cunts in there, but it was basically okay. I was expecting worse."

"What did you have to do?"

"Nothing I didn't want to," he said, with a slight edge. "I mean you couldn't drink, obviously. But there was no sport or anything. There was group, but I didn't do any of that. They can't make you.

Mainly I played Xbox. I read *Revolution in the Head* by Ian MacDonald, which was pretty good."

"How long were you there?"

"Two weeks."

"You were in rehab for two weeks and you never mentioned it?"

"It's not the sort of thing you go on about, pal."

"Even so . . . Christ."

"Anyway, I was there for a couple of weeks, and I started to sleep properly again, and it was the most amazing thing: I started to feel really good. My skin looked better, I was less puffy, my cheeks were taut. I felt taller, taller and thinner. And I felt clean. I shook their hands at the end of the treatment and went out into the street. And it was a beautiful summer's day, the sky was blue, and I could feel the sun on my shoulders. I felt like an animal emerging from hibernation. And there were women everywhere, beautiful women, with tanned skin and bare midriffs, and I felt sexy for the first time in living memory. I felt like I could be attractive, that I could have that quality, you know. And the girls were looking at me for the first time in years too, the way they used to. Eyes to the ground, shy smiles, fingers running through their hair. I felt new, like I'd been born again, like a Christian coming out of the swimming pool in a nighty. I hadn't felt so good in fucking years. It was like being young again. It was amazing."

"It sounds like it."

"You know what I did?" he said, smiling.

"No."

"I went to the pub." He looked away. I could see him smile. I couldn't read the smile.

"That's just who I am, Paul. That's who I am."

At some point I went to bed that night. When I padded through to the living room the next morning where I had left Brendan spark-out on the sofa, he was gone. There was a note written in his spidery hand on the coffee table. It read: "Sorry mate" and there was a large dark patch on the sofa. It stank, but I was in a hurry for work, so I sprayed some Fabreze on it and took a shower.

"Sorry mate".

It was the first time that Brendan had ever apologised for anything. Maybe he was growing as a person after all. I stood under the shower. It was a warm feeling.

HONEY WILD AND MANNA-DEW

I OFTEN DREAM about my dad. I don't know why as we weren't especially close. We weren't enemies, there was no bad feeling, but I always felt like a moon tethered to his orbit, never getting too near, respectfully distant. But I do often dream about him, and I never dream about my mum, though we were closer. I'm a man in my middle-years and a fair few people I've known have died and I don't dream about them either. Just my dad.

We get on well in the dreams, with the same slightly baffled relationship we had when he was alive. We weren't very alike. I was tall and thin he was short and stocky. My hair is brown, and his was jet black with a parting as perfect as a scar. The blackness wasn't entirely natural. His hair was always thick with pomade and crenulated where he fought hard against a natural curl. My hair's dead straight.

I dream we're in his shed, with its strange chemical smell and its rows of rusting tools hanging from nails in neat stripes. Can you smell in your dreams? I can't imagine the interior of that space *without* the smell. It was a simple fact, even in a dream so if I was dreaming about the shed there was going to be the shed smell. My dad had a rusted can of vegetable soup in a G-clamp on his workbench. He told me, in the disconnected manner of dream conversation, that he found the soup buried round the back of the shed. It was Army Surplus soup from the Second World War but "should be good to go" (*would my father have used the phrase?*). I couldn't believe he wanted to eat this ancient slop, abandoned for decades, semi-buried, but he grew up in the war and maybe he still had a taste for it. He attacked the brown, label-less tin (*how does he know there's soup in it?*) with a hammer and chisel, and suddenly I desperately wanted to leave, but it was too late. He'd forced a hole into the rim and the ancient soup had squirted, a thin noxious arc, that hit me in the face and filled my eyes, my mouth, my nose. I pawed at my face, but I couldn't see, my senses were overloaded with the filthy, clinging stink and the sound of my dad's helpless laughter.

Then the phone rang, and I woke up, licking my dry lips, glad to be gone from the dream. I knew it was my friend Scott calling as the ringtone was "Wonderful Life" by the band Black. Scott was the only person in my address book who had a bespoke ringtone because he had put it on my phone, and I didn't know how to get it off again. We were in the pub, and he rang me from the toilet to test if it worked. The phone started emitting a mournful synthesiser refrain and I answered, suspiciously.

"Hello?"

"Did it work?" said a voice.

"Did what work? Who is this?"

"The ringtone—did it work?"

"Is that you, Scott? Are you ringing me from the toilet?"

"Did it play the song?" Glee echoed in his voice.

" 'Wonderful Life' by Black?"

"Yeah."

"Yeah, it did."

"Brilliant."

"Is it going to do that every time it rings, Scott? I *quite* like the song . . ."

"Only when *I* ring you. It's our little ringtone." I heard a toilet flushing.

"Scott. Are you taking a shit while you're talking to me?"

"Not anymore."

He emerged beaming seconds later, his phone still in his hand. I vowed at that moment never to use his phone, not even in an emergency. This was Scott all over. He loved life and grabbed it with such wolfish vitality he rarely remembered to wash his hands.

He did seem to have a wonderful life. He was rich, had a beautiful wife, and his children looked like they'd had trials for the Vienna Boys Choir. He lived in a beautiful house, drove a sleek Italian car and had perhaps the most unnatural glow-in-the-dark teeth I'd ever seen. They floated through the pub's gloom with eerie phosphorescence, like the ghost of a vicar's collar. Scott never lost interest in life: that was his secret. If it was happening, whatever it was, he not only knew about it, but it impacted one of his many business concerns. He was a Zeitguy. I couldn't believe his energy and appetite. It was relentless. He guzzled the world like fire.

I let the phone ring off. Eight thirty on a Saturday morning. It was too much Scott too early. No doubt he'd been up since dawn baking bread or recording the dawn chorus or farting in a leotard with his supple wife.

The phone rang again. *It's a wonderful, wonderful life.* I pulled the pillow over my face, packing my ears with the edges. The fourth time he rang I picked it up. He was persistent.

"Verbo," he shouted. He was the only person who called me "Verbo". Most people got on fine with Paul.

"Didn't wake you, did I?"

"No, Scott," I said, "I was too excited to get any shut eye—it's only two hundred and fifty sleeps till Christmas."

"I love Christmas," he said. Sarcasm pinged off him.

"What do you want, Scott?"

"What are you doing tonight, mate?"

"Nothing."

As soon as I said it, I knew it was a mistake. This was why he phoned me so early—I was sloppy and still half asleep. Normally I'd have hedged my bets, kept an artful lie in reserve. Something to fall back on. Now I was adrift, naked and exposed.

"Great. Lucy and I are having one of our infamous soirees tonight. Fancy it?"

"This evening?" I said, weakly, "Oh, I thought you said last evening..."

"No, you didn't," he said.

"No, I didn't."

"So, eight o' clock tonight, then. Bring some wine, we'll do the rest."

"Right."

"Thinking of bringing anyone?"

"No."

"Great," he said, and rang off.

A dinner party, a fucking dinner party, and a last-minute invitation too. Somebody must have dropped out. I was making the numbers up. Thanks Scott. But that was only the best-case scenario, my preferred option. The alternative was this was a set up.

Scott and Lucy were a happy, handsome couple. They were the sort of family you saw in adverts smiling in elbow pads on bikes or freewheeling through mountain passes, kicking up gravel in an SUV. They had a large canvas portrait of themselves in the living room, each member of the family in white shirts, blue jeans and bare feet, hugging and smiling their immaculate smiles. They were people that lifestyle magazines were for and about. When people like that, people consumed by the trappings of their own happiness, have a pair of single friends it is their natural impulse to spread their joy. They want everyone to be as happy as they are, and to hell with the human cost. Love-blind people fail to understand fundamental things about the people they prey on. Their friends may be lacking in confidence, they might be awkward in social gatherings, they may prefer to rake their thighs with forks rather than make miserable small talk about the Marvel Extended

Universe under the dim light of a candle's flame and the brighter glare of their host's expectations. I rang Scott back immediately. He answered the phone, breathless.

"Scott," I said.

"Verbo," he said, whispering "It's Verbo" to a third party.

"You alright, mate?" I said, "you sound a bit out of breath."

"I'm making love to Lucy," he replied. I recoiled from the phone. My God.

"You stopped having sex with your wife to answer the phone?"

"I haven't *stopped*." There was some grunting and snuffling at this point. "Lucy says 'Hi' by the way."

"I'm hanging up," I said.

"What were you phoning for?"

"Oh God. This is hideous . . ."

"Thanks mate. I think it's . . . rather . . . urgh . . . beautiful."

"Look. Tonight. Is it a set-up?"

"How do you . . . me-ean?" he said, the last word strangely articulated. I *had* to hang up.

"Are you trying to fix me up with someone?"

"Not me. I'm not in the match-making business. What about you, darling?" I heard breathy denial from Lucy.

"She says no."

"Right."

"Do you want us t-oooo . . .?"

"No. You're fine. Seeyoutonightyesbye."

I hung up and took a long shower.

I arrived at Scott's fashionably on time. He lived twenty minutes away so I decided to walk, hoping to trip on a paving stone and chip a knee-bone so I could ring them, white with pain in the gutter, and tell them I could no longer make dinner. I didn't know what was wrong with me. Other people, if they didn't want to go to things, could just say no. They never gave it second thought. "Dinner? No, that sounds shit, ta ta," and off they went on their merry way, whistling and skimming stones. Why couldn't I do that? Why did I have to make everybody like me all the time? For one thing, it hadn't worked—I was not universally adored. So why make all this effort? Perhaps, on some unfathomable level, I really wanted to go to a dinner party and sit down next to someone and talk and maybe make some sort of connection and feel attractive and worthwhile, however briefly. Maybe that was it.

I made it to the house in one piece, as did the two bottles of Wolf Blass I carried. I knew these bottles would be appraised on the doorstep and spirited away, never to be seen again. Only Scott's good wine would make the table.

I trudged up the gravel of the freshly raked drive. The house was enormous. He had a lion's head door-knocker—well, of course he did—and I rapped it against the plate on the heavy wooden door.

They arrived as a couple, wreathed in smiles. Scott looked healthy and tanned. I ventured a hand, but he ignored it, requesting I "bring it in", which meant hugging him. Lucy also offered a hug and a couple of air kisses, and I tried not to think of Scott's penis being inside her mere hours ago. She smelled clean. I thrust the wine at her.

"Wolf Blass," she said, "great. Look Scott. Wolf Blass."

"Great. Cheers mate," said Scott.

What was wrong with Wolf Blass? If someone shows up with a bottle that costs north of a tenner you can't sniff at that. The bottles disappeared into the house to be hidden away. I wondered what they did with all the uncool wine guests brought them. Did they donate it to the homeless? Did they clean the silver with it?

I wandered into the house behind Lucy. She was gorgeous, so small and lithe, like a middle-aged ballerina. She was one of those effortless people. I couldn't imagine her hurt or confused or sweating. She was utterly self-contained, complete as a cat. I followed her into the house as Scott returned to the kitchen. He was an excellent cook. Of course, he was.

"Little aperitif, Paul?" Lucy said and poured me a needlessly complicated gin and tonic which had fruit and flowers bobbing around on top of its rose flavoured mixer. It was quite nice. She'd chipped the ice from a big block because even their ice was artisan. She gestured that I should go through to the living room while she saw how Scott was getting on. There was a couple in the living room: Jen and Dan. They were both blandly good-looking and tastefully dressed, and I'd never met either of them before. Dan did something in futures and Jen sat on the board of a few women's charities. I'm not sure whether that was a job or she did it for fun, but both these things sounded frightfully impressive, if you were the sort of person who was impressed by people's jobs. I'd been to these sorts of parties before and was a master of deflection when it came to talking about my own work. I simply do not engage. I could see this was upsetting for Dan who was desperate to put me in a box, but it was like trying to bathe a cat—I was not having it.

"So, what do you do, Paul?" said Dan. He was the sort of man who started sentences with "So . . ."

"Oh, you know. I get by."

"Get by doing what?"

"This and that."

"Yes, but what sort of this and that?"

"Oh, I love this song. Who is it?"

"I think its Massive Attack."

"Really? Those records don't really age, do they? Do you like music?"

"I suppose. Who doesn't like music?"

"You'd be surprised. I used to work with a guy who said he "didn't understand all the fuss about music."

"At your work?"

"Yeah, he was a total sociopath. You should have seen the notes he left in the fridge. He did a poo every day at exactly 11.25. Every single day. Once there was fire drill at 11.27 and the fire warden couldn't get him to leave the cubicle. He nearly got fired."

After briefly assimilating this information, Dan and Jen elected to change the subject. Victory was mine.

Lucy appeared at the door with two more guests, a tall blonde man with salmon-coloured jeans and a popped collar, and a small thin woman with dark hair. Lucy introduced the man as "Beans" but left before introducing the woman, after a cry for assistance from the kitchen. Dan and Jen instantly gravitated toward Beans, who lost no time talking about his job, and I was left on the sofa alone.

"Paul?"

It was Lucy again, hovering over me with a stranger. A female stranger. A female stranger who did not look one bit impressed.

"Paul, this is Miri. Miri, Paul. Can I leave her with you? I think I hear Scott calling me." She gave Miri a look, and Miri shot her one back that could have dented a Skoda. Great.

"Hi, Miri," I said, "I'm Paul."

"I know."

"How do you know, Lucy?"

"Christ. REALLY?"

"Shall we sit in silence ignoring each other?"

"Oh God, could we? Thank you."

"I'd prefer that," I said. We sat next to each other on the sofa, comfortably exiled from each other, staring at the rest of the party. Another couple wandered confidently into the room and joined Beans and Dan and Jen and the woman I hadn't been introduced to. The woman was Jax, and the man was called Paul. I later found out that I had been designated "Paul 2", even though I'd been here first.

Fine.

Scott appeared in his pinny, banging two saucepans together.

"Dinner is served. If you would like to follow your hostess into the dining room..."

"Paul 2," said Lucy, "why don't you sit next to Miri? We don't want you two at a loose end." The food looked amazing. Of course, it did. I had no idea what any of it was. Scott was on a Middle Eastern tip, and everything he cooked was presented in semi-glazed earthenware bowls and resembled creamy spiral galaxies.

"This looks amazing," said Beans and broke into applause. No one joined him but he didn't seem in the least embarrassed. I'm often amazed by other people's resilience. I didn't have to worry about not knowing what any of the food was, because Scott was keen to go into it all: where he'd sourced the ingredients, where the recipe came from geographically, and how he'd refined it. We started with an Iraqui Kitcharee, which was rice and lentils with a fried egg on it. Then there was spiced roast cauliflower with almonds and tahini dressing, which was a peppery cauliflower in some yoghurt. There was a lot of coriander. There was a side of Batatta Harra: chips with cayenne pepper and lemon juice and a load more coriander. Good job I like coriander.

There was a Baba Ghanouj, pulped aubergines, and chicken with pomegranate and beetroot tabbouleh, "a modern twist on a classic Mediterranean dish", according to Scott. Last came a Persian rice pudding with rosewater and cardamom syrup. Every dish was delicious, and Scott was in his element, flushed and grinning, expansive at the head of the table. There was something odd about him I couldn't quite place, until it struck me—this was the longest I'd seen him without a phone in his hand for twenty years. This was what Scott looked like when he was enjoying himself, this was Scott relaxing. He was present and centred, and the evening flowed through him. It was the exact opposite of how he was when he was out drinking with Brendan and me. I was slightly hurt. I thought he enjoyed *my* company at least. He seemed to. But this guy? This guy had his sleeves rolled up and he was telling stories and getting laughs. This guy had his coat off.

All through the meal Miri and I didn't exchange a word. There was no malice, at least not from me. We both knew what Lisa and Scott tried to do and neither of us wanted any part of it. Our eyes met briefly over the Baba Ghanouj, and we shared a grimace. I think if we'd met again under different circumstances, we might have been friends, but not here, not like this. You can't foster romance by pushing people together through trickery. There is instant, natural resistance. I was proud of us.

Sat on the other side of me was the girl I hadn't been introduced to. She was quite drunk already and Beans, who was her date, seemed far more interested in talking to Paul 1 and Jax, so I talked to her. She was jittery and funny and had two red wine ticks at the corner of her mouth. Her eyes were dark and intense and her hair black and heavy. She was very beautiful, actually. But so drunk.

I learned that she was on a date with Beans, whose name really did appear to be Beans. It was their second date and I also gathered, from the purple toothed smiles and heavy winks, that she didn't like him much. We briefly discussed films and she told me a few of her favourites—quite cool—but when she spilled a glass of pinot the entire length of the table, Beans elected, after a great deal of prissing and fussing, to take her home.

"Bye Paul," she said as she left, "nice meeting you."

"Bye," I said, realising I still didn't know her name. Looking around the table, I resolved to follow her example, draining a few glasses in quick succession, as no one was talking to me anymore. I soon became extremely annoyed by Paul 1.

"You stole my name," I said, waving a finger at his shiny, pink blur of a face.

"What, mate?"

"I'm Paul 1. You're Paul 2. I was here first. Stands to reason."

"Alright," he said slowly and reasonably, in a manner designed to infuriate me.

"You can be Paul 1 then. I'll be Paul 2. It's no skin off my teeth."

"Nose," I said.

"Paul," said Scott.

"Nose," I repeated, with venom. "It's 'no skin off my nose'. You get things done 'by the skin of your teeth.' It's a completely different idiom for a completely different situation." I banged the table with my fist.

"Is he alright?" said Jax to Scott.

"He's fine," said Scott.

"Do you want a little lie down," said Lucy. He beautiful eyes seemed concerned.

"You should have studied ballet," I said.

"I did," she replied, "for years. In Paris."

"I knew it."

"Would you like a little lie down, Paul?"

"You will not make me go to my basket," I said standing up confidently, falling back into my seat and then climbing up again, hesitantly, and clinging to the table. "I am not your lap dog, Lucy. I shall leave. I know when I've been insulted. And it was at some point this evening. Where's my *Wolf Blass*? I'm taking it home. What's wrong with *Wolf Blass* anyway? Timothy Findley used to drink it—he's a writer you never heard of. He probably hated Baba Ghanouj."

"I'll call you a taxi, mate," said Scott, while Lucy went to get the bottles of wine.

"No thanks," I said, "I need some air. A lot of air. All I can get. I will be drunk on air. Paul 2, goodnight. Miri, thank you for not talking to me. Most refreshing."

I scooped the carrier bag from Lucy's hand, which I then kissed. I looked soulfully into her eyes.

"You're very beautiful," I said. I turned to Scott. "Bring it in, mate," I said, and he did so, reluctantly.

"You're a lucky man, Scott, a lucky man. No . . ." I had a sudden realisation, "No, you've *made* your luck. You're a brilliant man, beautiful in your own way. You deserve her. I mean that." I kissed him on the cheek and went out of the room. I could hear Miri applauding and laughing as I left.

In the cool night air, the full extent of my drunkenness hit me with sudden violence, and the journey, however long it took, was dispersed in the shaken snowstorm of my memory. The next thing I remembered was fatigue setting in as I toiled at my front door, my key too fat for the lock. After what seemed hours, something finally took, the key found purchase, a click and I stumbled into my hallway. Another few minutes got me into the flat proper, where I kicked off my shoes but didn't bother to undress, falling onto the bed and lying there on my back.

I think it went okay. I got a bit drunk, but I didn't do anything unforgivable. I kissed the hostess and hugged the host. I might have been rude to Paul 2 but fuck Paul 2. I started to drift. I hadn't met anyone. What would have happened if I had hit it off with Miri? Or with the girl whose name I didn't know. I had to be a better bet than fucking Beans. Ah well, it hadn't happened. Maybe it was never ever going to happen. It wasn't going to happen. If it was going to happen it would have already happened. I was old and fat and ugly and would not improve. I would lie here and stare at the ceiling, perhaps forever. This was fine.

There was an insistent rhythmic noise from upstairs. The sound of headboard meeting wall. The woman upstairs was having sex. Good for her, I thought, as I succumbed to sleep. Good for her. I'm glad someone was.

The Proudest Boast

NEIL HOVERED over my desk.

"Paul, sorry, could you sign this card for Carol?"

"Sorry, Neil," I said, "I don't have her power of attorney."

He registered this with a flicker of the eye.

"No. The card is *for* Carol. I don't need you to sign it *as* Carol."

I sighed. "Just give me the card, Neil."

I signed Carol's card, placing a kiss at the end of my "best wishes" even though I didn't much like her, and Neil whisked it away to bother another bank of desks. While he was standing there, he gave me a sharp look and said something to Fay and Yasmine and all three of them laughed.

Fine.

I'd gone off Neil. Neil was gay and when I'd been told I was going to have a gay man working under me I was delighted, so delighted in fact I didn't crack the obvious jokes that immediately occurred to me.

As a man in his fifties who was born in the sixties, I was literally a child of the Summer of Love. The baby boomers instituted free love, perfected the pop form and broke down all social norms (or said they did, the women were still making the tea and cleaning the bath). Short backs and sides grew out, de-mob suits were replaced by velvet jackets and beads, and everything was loosened. Sex didn't have to make you pregnant anymore, drugs were no longer the preserve of jazz musicians, and you didn't have to look like your parents, live like your parents or listen to your parents. The world was brand new, fresh as paint.

Obviously that mainly happened in Chelsea or the Kings Road, and the rest of the UK was still as grey and narrow as it had always been. None of which explains what I see of my generation, the children of the Summer of Love. Those changes happened, the genie was out of the bottle, you couldn't stuff it back in again. But what they chose to do was just ignore it, apparently. I looked at the people, the men, of my generation, the rows of gammon squatting on the Question Time benches, simmering gently, their jowls a-quiver, espousing views that my parents would think were a bit unreconstructed. And my parents were jerry-built.

I mean I'm younger than Björk. How can anyone younger than Björk still be racist, sexist and homophobic? She's a magical space pixie sent to tell us that mythology is real, that science is magic, and you can puncture the walls of reality if you just shout hard enough at them. And she's been on the planet longer than these bald, bilious balls of pent-up rage. I like to think I'm not like these people. I'm tolerant. No, not tolerant, I'm actively open to different cultures or sexualities or gender definitions. I'm making inroads into calling people "they" if that's what they want. Fuck it—whatever makes them happy. It's like putting on glasses with a new prescription. You take a while to adjust and then its fine.

Which brings me back to Neil. Neil's gay and I don't like Neil. I don't dislike him because he's gay, at least I don't think I do. I dislike him because he's a little shit. But maybe his sexuality is part of it. I'm not sure he's gay *enough*. He's ordinary—boring, snide and dull. I like my homosexuals flamboyant, outrageous and slyly predatory. Or at least I imagine I do. Might get a bit tiring after a while, possibly almost immediately. But I've never really met any gay guys like that. The ones I meet are badly dressed men with ketchup stains on their ties who happen to like a bit of cock. I wanted glamour, excitement, cattiness, descriptions of extraordinarily slutty behaviour that I could roll my eyes at, but secretly be impressed by. What I got was Neil. Neil, whom I could see picking his nose by the printer. Neil, who undermined me in meetings, and I was pretty sure once did that thing of coughing the word "wanker" as I was making a presentation. It didn't matter to me where he wanted to put his penis, he was just a nasty little shit in a shitty suit and shitty pointy brown shoes.

So, when he invited me to Carol's leaving do and I said yes, I think we were both a bit surprised. We sat with our backs turned away from each other on the pub banquette. Neil presided over most of the room and regaled them with heroic tales of the boxsets he had "done" over the weekend. He really was quite the raconteur. Peter Ustinov must have been spinning in his grave.

I was talking to a German girl who was doing work experience in the office. Tina was 19, hoping to improve her English, and didn't drink. I was on my fourth pint and couldn't think of anything to say. She was wearing a big, puffy all-weather jacket, the sleeves of which had swallowed her hands to the fingertips. There were two badges on her coat: one depicted a hot dog and the other Magritte's "C'est si ne pas une pipe", his portrait of a pipe that he was saying wasn't a pipe because it was a picture of a pipe. An important point and well worth making. When in doubt always say what you see.

"Ce'st si ne pas une pipe," I said.

She smiled and nodded.

"Magritte," I said.

"Yes."

"Rene Magritte," I said.

She nodded.

"I like Magritte," I said.

"Me also," she said, "this is why I wear the button."

I was momentarily confused.

"Badge!" I said, suddenly and loudly. Neil half turned and gave Saskia and Dionne a sort of pout, which made them laugh. I ignored him.

"Badge," I said again, "in the UK we say badge not button. Button is American."

"Badge?"

"Like badger," I added, unhelpfully, "but without . . . the er . . . on the end of it . . ."

My voice trailed off and she looked bored, sipping on lime and soda. I looked for something to say but all I could see were the two badges: a hot dog and not a pipe. The two disparate objects brushed up against one another on the dissecting table of my mind, until I had a moment of white-hot inspiration.

"Ich bin kein Frankfurter!" I shouted.

"He's finally lost it," said Neil. Laughter. Tina went to get another soda-water from the bar, and I talked to Tim from Actuarial about *Black Mirror*.

I couldn't let it go. It burned inside me. I'd made an effort. I'd made an elegant and sophisticated joke, in another language yet. I had to get some credit for it. I was a middle-aged man talking to a girl less than half my age, and now she and the rest of the department thought I was bewildered. I had to strike back on behalf of failing codgers everywhere, I had to make them realise mine was the most supple and adventurous mind in the room.

Tim was in mid-flow, but I excused myself and went and sat down next to Tina, who looked slightly alarmed. Tim barely blinked. I imagine people walk off when he is talking to them quite regularly.

"Hi Tina," I said.

"Hello, Mr Reverb," she said.

"It's Paul when I'm out of the office."

"Okay."

"I wanted to explain about earlier. The badges."

"They are not buttons."

"Yes. I mean no, they aren't buttons, but I wanted to say that before, when I said "Ich bin kein Frankfurter" I wasn't just being mad. It was a joke—about John F Kennedy."

"Who?" said Neil.

Seriously. *Who is John F Kennedy?* What the fuck are they teaching them in school these days? He wouldn't last five minutes on "Pointless".

"The American President?" said Tina. "He was shot in the head?"

"Exactly," I said, turning to look scornfully at Neil. "You see, Neil? She knows."

Neil shrugged and his little group of friends laughed.

Fine.

"Okay," said Tina. She pushed her glasses up the bridge of her nose and I could see that her large blue eyes were worried. Shit. I determined to explain the joke as quickly as possible. Then we could all laugh, accept my cleverness, and move on.

"The President was addressing the people of Frankfurt in the early '60s..."

"Before they shot him!" said Neil. Ripples of laughter.

"... and he delivered this famous speech where he declared 'Ich bin ein Frankfurter' which was roundly mocked in the German press because it meant 'I am a hotdog'. And I saw your hotdog badge and your Rene Magritte badge, and I blended the pair of them to come up with 'Ich bin kein Frankfurter'. And that was the joke!"

There was a brief silence. It was the kind of silence that anticipated either applause or people throwing things. Instead, it was punctured, as I knew it would be, by Neil.

"Well, I wouldn't open with it," he said.

"I don't think I understand," said Tina, "the president said he was a hotdog?"

"Yes. He didn't mean to—he accidentally said he was a hotdog, by mistake."

"In a speech?" said Tina.

"Yes, the president was an accidental hot dog in his speech."

"I don't really . . ."

"Donut," said Tim. Everyone turned to look at him. Tim was a thin, balding man with his tie loose at his throat.

"Donut," he said.

"Have I done something to upset you, mate?" I said. Neil and his friends giggled like they were at the back of a bus.

"Kennedy said 'Ich bin ein Berliner' because he was in Berlin not Frankfurt. A Berliner is the name of a kind of filled pancake. What he actually said was 'I am a donut.'"

Everyone turned to look at me. Tim was right. It was Berlin not Frankfurt. I looked at Tina's stupid hot dog badge, hating it. The bastard thing had fooled me, it had made me misremember a popular historical vignette and look foolish in front of a teenage girl and, worst of all, it had given Neil exactly the sort of ammunition he needed. I could see him now in my peripheral vision, his eyes wide, his mouth a perfect "o".

"Oh yes," said Tina, "I think I remember that now. That's quite funny."

Later that night as I perused the internet with a glass of wine in my hand, I found out that Tim's story had largely been discredited. In fact, the German press at the time had been very positive about the American president declaring spiritual unity with the capital so soon after the end of the Second World War.

The donut story came much later and didn't even work as a joke. I'd copied and pasted the relevant Wikipedia entry into an e mail to send to Tim cc-ing in Neil and Tina, but before I sent it, I deleted it.

Because . . . what was the fucking point?

Love Story (You and Me)

Silvia's on her uppers. She's had a fall and I'm at her house, butlering.

"There's an orange bag upstairs. Could you fetch it for me? It's in the little room."

Silvia no longer uses the top two floors of her house. I go upstairs to the little room. The little room is a repository of decades of undisturbed crap, piles piled on top of piles, a delicate eco-system with no visible means of support. It's like a dusty *Kerplunk*—one wrong move and the whole thing could avalanche on top of me. I hold my breath, but there's no sign of an orange bag. I go to the landing to call her and remember she's deaf and run down the stairs again.

"There's no orange bag."

"Have you *looked*?" she says.

"Yes, I've looked. There's no orange bag."

"Really?" she says with that mystified tone she uses when one of her speculations hasn't paid off.

"It's my clothes from the hospital. I could have sworn someone told me they had put them there, in an orange bag."

"Who would have told you that?"

"Oh, no idea," she says with a shrug, already bored.

"Could they be in your bedroom?"

"Could be." She is no longer looking up from her book.

I look in the bedroom. No orange bag.

"It's not in your bedroom," I say.

"This is really weird," she says, "I suppose they're just lost."

I go upstairs. There's an orange bag on the bed in the big room. Next to it is a pile of clothes, neatly folded. I don't know what to do. I don't know why she wants a bag of clothes. I realise I haven't done enough close questioning before starting out on this endeavour and now I'm paying the price. I go downstairs again.

"Right, I've found the orange bag. It was in the big bedroom."

"What was it doing in there?"

"I don't know."

"Who told me it was in the little bedroom, then?"

"I don't know."

"Strange."

She eyes me and I realise that I have become both the liar who lied about the whereabouts of the bag and the smug debunker who has exploded that lie. Clearly, I'm up to something.

"Do you want the bag?" I say.

"Yes, of course."

"It's been unpacked."

"Who did that?" The weirdness is really stacking up now. I go upstairs and carefully pack the clothes into the orange bag and then bring it down to her.

"What do you want me to do with it?" I ask.

"Give it here. Pop it next to me."

I look at her, in the little nest she has fashioned from blankets, paperbacks and the balled tissues she produces from her sleeves with the economy of a stage magician. There is a small table next to the sofa upon which rests the following: her glasses, her glasses case, several more paperback books, a mug with lipstick smudged around the brim, her purse, her diary, her address book, her prayer cards, the television remote control, the DVD remote control, the video remote control, and another remote control which might be for a previous DVD player, and all of this in a space no larger than a chess-board. On the sofa next to her are more books, a blanket and a cardigan. Into this jumble sale she wants introduce a bag-for-life full of laundry.

"What are your ultimate plans for this bag, Silvia?"

"I'm going to unpack it and fold it properly."

"And once that's happened where will you put the clothes?"

"In the bedroom."

"So, to recap: you want me to fetch a bag from a specific location, but it turns out, in fact, that the bag wasn't in that location. I then go to the most likely location, but the bag isn't there either. A subsequent investigation reveals the bag to be in another room with its contents neatly folded on the bed, and now you want me to carefully place the clothes back into the bag, take it to you so you can unpack it, refold it, replace it in the bag, so I can take it into another room and unpack it again."

"I suppose so," she pouts.

"Would it not have been quicker to say to me 'Somewhere in this house there is a large orange bag with clothes either in it or near it. Find it and put it in my bedroom.'"

"I don't know why you bother coming here if you're just going to pick fights with me."

She's a tiny figure on the sofa, surrounded by her familiar things, each ergonomically worn to her touch. She's like a Saxon noblewoman, buried with treasures in easy reach, ready for the afterlife. She'd kill me for calling her a Saxon.

Her foot is up on the leather footrest that I assembled for her. It is swollen and she sweats trapped water through her pores, so the hem of her slacks is moist to the touch. There are no breaks in the skin but there are patches where the membrane seems to be stretched too thin, the meat of her pressing hard for rupture. Her toes are sausages that need pricking, tripe white and irregular, and straying off at angles. It is the result, she claims, of wearing high heels for a half century. Her skin quivers at the jawline and her chin is blanched white with indignation. I'm annoyed at an old woman who wants me to check her laundry's folded. That's all. I'm the worst man in the world.

"I'm sorry," I say, "it's just all the running about. I'm knackered. It's boiling here."

"It's 'cause you're fat," she says. "If it wasn't for that . . ." she points at my stomach ". . . you'd be fine. I thought you'd *swallowed* my laundry."

She starts to laugh and immediately looks 20 years younger. Colour fills in her cheeks beneath her gypsum mask. She has found the secret of eternal youth—being rude to me.

I soak it up. Fat lads do. She looks so happy.

Silvia lives on the bottom floor of her house. She could afford a stair-lift but doesn't want one as she's given up on the other two floors. Like the son she doesn't speak to, she's no longer at home to two thirds of her house.

When I'm staying with her, I sleep in one of the bedrooms on the second floor. It's a forgotten world. An old school desk is filled with her son's schoolbooks (terrible penmanship). There are fat, squat televisions and dusty dark-wood furniture. In one of the bedrooms, I found piles of greenish coppers stacked carelessly in towers, all of which pre-dated decimalisation. I barely pre-date decimalisation.

None of the hot taps in the house work, so I've been boiling the kettle to do the washing up. It's also quite difficult to wash myself, which is problematic as her house is roasting hot. The atmosphere is so soupy and sleepy you could cultivate orchids here. Silvia's not keen on orchids as she has enough Latin to know they're named after testicles. I bought her a bunch once and she accused me of presenting her with a "vase full of bollocks".

The hot tap in the tub does work and, while she has an afternoon snooze, I elect to have bath. Her bath is small, practically ovoid, and there's carpet on the bathroom floor. I place my hand on the towel rail as I dip a toe into the water, and it immediately gives way. I replace it in its loose holder—I don't have to worry—its upstairs, and she will never venture upstairs.

Gingerly stepping into the bath, I ease myself under the water, my knees pressed to my chest. I pick up a bottle of shampoo, but it's empty. I pick up some shower gel and the plastic crumbles at the base, decayed and brittle. How long does it take for plastic to break down? Decades? How long has this stuff been here? How long have they been making shower gel?

Silvia has a cleaner, but she only does two hours a week and that's barely enough time to sweep up the topsoil. I've been here five days already, and I've barely scratched the surface. The grease on the hood of the hob defies all known cleaning practice. I've hit it with every product in the cupboard and it laughs at my foolish efforts. I may have got the first ten layers off, but the sponge still refuses to move smoothly over the tacky wood laminate. An oxy-acetylene torch might be the only language it understands. The grease's provenance is mysterious too, as Silvia never cooks. I genuinely don't know what she eats beyond porridge and wine. Silvia's a mysterious person generally, and the mystery deepens daily. She's inscrutable, swathed in fabric like a winding-sheet, with someone else's leg propped up before her, as big as she is small. She's ingrained on the sofa, stubborn as a stain.

We don't talk about the accident, that's understood. It happened late at night and traditionally she is fond of a nightcap or two. She was lucky—she fell the night before the cleaner came. If it had happened the night after she might have been there a week. At least she doesn't have a cat. I imagine the cleaner opening the door to find her eviscerated corpse on the living room floor, the soft meat of her powdery cheeks torn away while Tiddles looks fat and guilty in the corner of the room.

But there's no Tiddles and I'm the guilty one. I hardly ever visit. She calls me "The Equinox", as I show up twice a year. Which is why I've elected to move in with her while she's recovering: it's the guilt. She certainly doesn't want me here. She likes her privacy. She doesn't want anyone to know how she lives. And I don't want to know either. It's a burden. I'm in on her secret even though neither of us wants me to be. I feel obliged to help now. There's stuff to do.

I get out of the bath and find I like the soft carpet under my wet feet. I root around in the cabinet over the sink. There's a shampoo that hasn't turned to dust. It's for damaged hair and has a hint of lilac, but I'll risk it for now. I can get down to Londis tomorrow and pick up some Head and Shoulders. The heat is drying my scalp and I'm wearing epaulettes of desiccated human skin.

I'm terrified for her. She's small and brittle and suddenly so hungry for life. She's urgent. She has a walker now, what they used to call a Zimmer frame. It has a plastic tub on the front of it so she can fetch and carry things. It's industrial grey and functional and she uses it to transport bowls of soup or cereal from the kitchen and back to her nest on the sofa. It's constantly full of residue, as she judders along her short journeys. There is a fat stripe of unidentifiable gunk around the base like the ribbon on a birthday cake. Every step is a stutter, her eyes fixed on a distant point, her shoulders square against another of gravity's sneak attacks. A month ago, she was fine, her posture good and her conversation reassuringly waspish. She seems to have aged twenty years since leaving the hospital. Before she was an immortal: my aunt, always and forever, an immutable fact. She would always be there. Now she seemed to be fighting every second just to stay in the world, every thud of the walker's rubber stopper is a crampon hammered into rock, without which she would fall away, gone from the earth.

She's my family. She's it. When she dies, and it suddenly seems she might, that's it for my line. The name will die with me. Reverb.

It's a stupid name and perhaps it deserves to die. Last of the Reverbs. That doesn't sound even slightly magnificent. I die without issue, of course. My books were meant to have been my children, but I didn't ever finish one. A vampire hypnotist. My God. I shall die as I've lived—the customer services manager for a middling insurance company. I don't even have a policy with them. I did have one, but I cashed it in and bought a home-studio so I could carry on with my musical career. I was in my late thirties then and between girlfriends, so no one talked me out of it. The cusp of forty is too old to be a pop star but there are ways of making music even when you're old. And really, from this distance your thirties are hardly old. But I haven't touched the studio. It sits there gathering dust, next to the telecaster in its stand with its price tag still on. I should give these things away. I'm hoarding them. Other people would love this stuff, but I'm squatting on it like a lazy dragon in a cave full of ingots.

Silvia stomps back from the toilet.

"You going to make yourself useful?" she gasps.

She's putting a brave, perfectly made-up face on it, but it is obvious these journeys are exhausting her. When she finally sits down on the sofa she doesn't move for a full minute. She sits there with her eyes clamped shut. She looks as if she is holding her breath, but her chest moves in and out rapidly. She's like animal cornered after a chase.

She wants me to put a film on for her. We continue to watch films together, none made this century, which suits me. I'm in retreat from the twenty first century. I don't like anything about it. The cinema, the music, the politics, the people. It's an ugly, fevered place, a derelict playground for the id. Nothing is unspoken any more. British people used to be reserved and repressed, we were wonderful hypocrites. How I miss hypocrisy. What a fabulous British institution—we built an empire on it. I think of repression fondly, like a good friend who died young. I envy the people of the past, the secrecy of their lives and the way oppressive class distinctions policed them. Nowadays when people sneeze, they show you the contents of their handkerchiefs. They take a dump and offer you a guided tour of the bathroom without flushing. I don't want to know that your relationship status is "complicated, and I don't want to see pictures of your operation-scar, no matter how many filters you put on it.

We're watching a film called *The House in the Woods*. Michael Gough and Patricia Roc rent a house in the middle of a forest from an eccentric sculptor who neglects to move out. The sound is very poor on the film print and, because Silvia demands the volume is on maximum all the time, the parts where the sound erodes sound like screeds of white noise. It's like looking at pictures of Pat Roc during a My Bloody Valentine gig which, in all honestly, sounds like a good night out.

Patricia Roc is a beautiful woman. A quick calculation tells me she is forty-two in this film, but she looks half that. But at least she's age appropriate. I find myself increasingly attracted to actresses whose careers were over before I was born. She was born twenty-five years before Silvia. I don't really want to delve too deeply into what any of this might mean psychologically, but Patricia Roc, Joan Fontaine, Googie Withers, how blithe they seem, how strangely modern. Joan Fontaine's entire career is based on ironic suffering. Googie Withers—what a name—is simultaneously ancient and modern: a face suited to a Pharaonic headdress, a mop cap or a hoodie.

The film is short, and I have no idea what or whom it was made for. It looks barrel-scrapingly cheap. There are about three locations, and the fight scene at the end looks like it was edited by feeding the film stock into a bacon slicer. Silvia and I have watched it about fifteen times together and she never misses an opportunity to say, "The sound on this is terrible", when the audio starts to degrade. She likes the film because this is an understandable England. Michael Gough is a writer who's had a bad war. Nevertheless, he can afford a fashionable North London flat and a jeep. Pat Roc, beaming like a domesticated sun, doesn't seem to do anything except manage Gough's mood swings in a relentlessly upbeat manner. Later, when she meets the artist, whom you can tell is Bohemian and a bad hat because he has a beard and espouses Nietzschean philosophy worryingly close to the end of the Second World War, she tries to fix him too. At their first meeting he immediately asks her husband for permission to paint her. This never fails to get a hoot of derision from Silvia.

"Why not ask *her*?" she sneers. "So much for modern art!"

The film is sixty years old.

Silvia's no feminist, at least she would tell you she isn't, but nothing gets her hurling abuse at the television more than men talking over women. I'm not sure it ever happened to her in her life, but she is ever vigilant on behalf of the meeker members of her sex. This may well be the secret of her affection for these old films, that deep well of patrician smugness harpooned from the comfort of the sofa. These competent, occasionally damaged men are benignly sexist. They look after and adore women, but never listen to them. It's an odd, privileged, powerless and sexless condition. To be on a pedestal with nobody daring to look up your skirt.

Silvia was in her mid-twenties when the Beatles first single came out, which is a matter of little importance to her. The swinging sixties happened to other people. Her sixties were dinner parties and classical concerts and wearing gloves when she went out. And when she went out, she went to clubs that hadn't changed in forty years. Her husband had been a pilot and most of her friends were the wives of his friends. Silvia being Silvia made sure they didn't stay friends for long. Even when she was young, Silvia was pass-remarkable to the point of assault. It was said her husband, Peter, requested long-haul flights on purpose. He retired in his mid-fifties and was dead in two years. According to the family it was death by a thousand cuts, the steady drip, drip, drip of Silvia's acid tongue. She had lost a lot of that power now, but remained incensed by bumptious masculine idiocy. Jeremy Clarkson was a special target for scorn.

"Look at him," she would say as the motoring journalist mugged his way through another episode of "Who Wants to Be a Millionaire", "sat there in his dead men's shoes."

"Chris Tarrant isn't dead, Silvia."

"Don't be stupid, Paul, I know. It's just this car idiot isn't half the man Tarrant is."

Pause.

"Though Tarrant's an arsehole too, of course. That's a perm."

"I don't think so."

"Oh, and I suppose Martin Shaw doesn't have a perm?"

"He doesn't anymore."

"Do I mean Michael Kitchen?"

"I no longer know."

"One cheekbone."

"I . . . can't imagine what that means."

"He has one cheekbone. Martin Shaw."

I left it there, but Martin Shaw *does* have one cheekbone. She was right. She was almost always right.

It made me feel good. She was always rude to me, Silvia, always had been. I think that's why I didn't see her for twenty years. If she told you what she thought of you she was always right. She got to the nub of the thing. You couldn't argue. Lately she has only teased me about my weight. The rest of me gets a pass. She often seems quite sad I'm alone.

"I wish you had someone, Paul. You'd be good for someone."

"Thanks, Silvia."

"Some plain little girl who wouldn't complain."

"Thank you very much."

"You know what I mean. Someone nice. Not too demanding."

"You don't think I can deal with demands?"

No words. A look.

"I thought you were dead against that sort of thing," I said. "Quiet, compliant women."

She shrugged.

"You wouldn't do them any harm. Girls like that should have someone like you. Save them from all the bastards."

We sat in silence for a while until I spilled a drop of wine, and she reversed her opinion of me, claiming that I would be alone until I died, as I pressed kitchen roll into the thick, pale carpet.

Son of Obituary

"Would you like to say a few words?"

Brendan's brother was frowning at me, the taut lines of his face drawing me to his narrow mouth. He was moon grey, the freckles that peppered his nose charcoal splinters.

"Not really, Conal," I said. "It's not my place."

"You're a writer, aren't you?" he said.

This surprised me.

"Unpublished," I said.

"Brendy always called you 'the writer' when he was talking about you."

"Yeah, I think he was being sarcastic," I said.

"No, I don't think so. You know Brendy: call a cunt a cunt."

"Did he ever call me a cunt?"

"Will you say a few words?" said Conal again. He was a tall, intense man. A cigarette shivered in his fingers; the nails were bitten to nothing.

"Of course. When?"

"The eulogy," he said, simply.

"You're joking."

He wasn't joking. I got the feeling that towering, glowering Conal, whom I noticed had some very unprofessional looking tattoos on his fingers, rarely joked. Somehow, I agreed to read the eulogy at Brendan's funeral.

I hadn't found his body. I was sulking, in fact. He'd paid a visit to my house and been sick in my tagine pot and hadn't told me, hiding it under the sink. I hadn't found it for three days, though the smell was evident almost immediately. I ignored his subsequent texts. I had already blocked him on social media for various other transgressions. He'd come round one evening, banging on the front door and I'd pretended to be out. I could still hear his voice as he shouted through my letterbox: long and low and forlorn, the stupid single syllable of my name. I would have forgiven him. I always forgave him. But that was the last time I heard his voice and I had to live with that now.

He died about three days later. He was found by a girl called Abigail whom I didn't know. Drug overdose. I didn't know he was still doing them. Brendan had small pockets of friends all over town and he didn't like them to mix. I didn't find that out until after he died, but here we all were. Strange metropolitan faces, stricken in the sticks.

It was a good turnout. His parents were small, Irish and brave, arms eventually around each other. His brother was stiff and distant, cold with grief. His wife and children kept their distance from him. He didn't seem safe. All his other brothers were there too, gangly, gaunt, spade-like chins resting on their chests, murmuring like pigeons. I couldn't understand how this Brobdingnagian brood had sprung from the loins of that silvery hobbit couple. The elderly Irish shrank like blisters.

I hid in the toilet to write. I had my notebook with me because I always had my notebook with me. I had about twenty minutes to sum up Brendan's life, twenty minutes of thumps on the toilet door while I tried to think of something nice to say about my best friend. They all knew him. They knew what he was like. It would be pointless soft-soaping them. And yet it was his funeral. People were crying. People had loved him, the best they could, in often ludicrous circumstances.

Besides Conal looked dangerous and I didn't want to say anything that might piss him off.

I could think of nothing. Or rather I could not see past what Brendan had become, all the lies, the bad grace.

And I couldn't see past the fact that he may have killed himself. May have. Not proven. He had, it turned out, recently broken his wrist in one of his falling over incidents. He'd stopped bouncing. He could no longer laugh off his little accidents. Fear made him brittle, and he snapped, bone dry. He'd got hold of some opiates— provenance unknown. He wouldn't have gone to a doctor. He hated doctors and comedians equally, both telling him how to feel.

He may have messed up his dosage, forgotten what he'd taken, while self-medicating for the pain. He may have been drinking even more than usual for the same reason. Or maybe he wanted to kill himself. There was always that uncertainty, he was Schrodinger's corpse. He would have hated me saying that. He would have told me that I was misusing the term, and that I didn't understand it. He'd be right. I was probably only using it to annoy him, goading a dead man, finally getting the last word. Literally, as I was writing his eulogy.

I could hear "Blue Jay Way" playing in the church. Brendan would be in there. In a box, in a suit, his mouth glued shut. The only way I'd be able to get through the speech without being heckled.

I'd seen him, briefly, before the service, before Conal had ushered me into the vestry and I had hidden in the toilet to write. His cheeks had been blushed and his nose was pale, the eyelashes were long and black. His hair had been artfully combed back and an attempt had been made to get the tobacco stain off it. He looked a lot like the old Brendy except he was relaxed, at peace. He'd finally stopped fidgeting. In life his legs were always swinging, feet kicking, fingers knotting and unravelling, jaw setting and unsetting. He had been a blur of nervous agitation. He was in the box like a ventriloquist's dummy, and I half expected to hear him kicking away at the lid.

Someone rapped sharply on the toilet door.

"Paul? You in there?" It was Conal's voice.

"Yeah, mate."

"Hurry it up, would you? You're on."

I looked down at my notes. I had nothing at all.

"Can you give me another five minutes, Conal?"

"I can give you a smack in the mouth."

I would have to busk it.

Fine.

Conal escorted me into the church from the vestry and I meekly stepped onto the altar and up the short flight of steps to the pulpit. Behind me was a board with a selection of hymn numbers on it. In front of me were three rows of Brendan's grieving family, each looking like an odd, distended version of him, a hall of mirrors reflecting futures that Brendan would never see, ghosts of his unspent lives. It was ghoulish, this melting waxworks, unpainted and grey, lined up in rows like tufty coconuts at a shy.

Beyond them were people I didn't know, Brendan's other friends. The only person I recognised was Scott, sitting right at the back in a beautiful black suit. He was looking at his phone and I found it oddly comforting.

I cleared my throat. The priest studiously studied the thick red carpet, his hands clasped in front of him. I'd get no help from him.

Fine.

I looked over at still, quiet Brendan. His coffin was a honey-coloured wood and reminded me of a pencil case I'd had at school. It had a sliding lid and was long enough to hold a six-inch ruler. And here was my mate Brendy resting in the six-foot version, his forehead dulled by matte powder, where mine was starting to shine under the church's lights.

"And now Brendan's friend Paul is going to say a few words on behalf of the family," the priest said, like a nudge in the ribs. He had a radio mic, which I thought was a bit much. I cleared my throat again.

"Thank you," I said, not knowing why. I had nothing.

"Brendan," I said. "Brendan. Brendan Joyce. My friend, Brendan. Friendan."

I let that sink in.

"I met Brendan when I was 15 years old," I continued. "That's over thirty-five years of friendship. We've both seen some ups and downs: when his marriage broke up, I was there for him. And when my parents died, I was there for him. We never actually talked about any of these things, we just got drunk together—that's what men do. We drink and we ignore the situation completely. Brendan and I have rarely, if ever, been sober in each other's company. Booze has been the lubrication for all our awkward meetings, smoothing the rough edges off his difficult personality."

There was a stirring in the room.

"*Our* difficult personalities."

I changed tack.

"Brendan Joyce was the cleverest man I've ever known. His was a truly dazzling array of gifts. There was nothing he couldn't turn his hand to. It was annoying when I first knew him and later, when he'd squandered his gifts like a lottery winner, it was infuriating. I've known Brendan for well over half my time on earth. He was part of the furniture of my life, one of those people who you've always known, the ones you never needed to see. You could go years and pick up again straight away, the old rhythms in place, the old in-jokes, all the shorthand that marks out true friendship.

"You think these people are commonplace, you think the people who have furnished your life for decades will always be there, that they are played out, known. They aren't. They're little worlds, delicate eco-systems constantly on the edge of collapse. They're pennies in an arcade waiting to drop off the shelf. You never really know anyone and the best you can do, if you love them, is to keep asking them questions, to open the lines of communication, to keep them talking."

I didn't know what I was saying at this point. The words kept forming and tumbling out. I wasn't checking to hear if they made sense, but they sounded alright as they whizzed past.

"I wish we'd talked more, Brendan and I, talked about something that mattered—not the Beatles, or some bullshit science thing or the size of the barmaid, the server's, tits. Or talked about his bloody stupid leg kicking up and down all the time, like a begging dog. But we didn't. We never talked about anything useful and now he's gone.

"Brendan was never easy. But I shall miss the difficulty. I shall miss the embarrassment. I'll miss all the apologies and the twisted knot of rage in my gut. Because of him, and because of what he did. I shall miss my stupid, wonderful, infuriating friend. He's wasted dead. He's no good dead."

I'd started to cry at some point. I wasn't sure when. I'd also closed my eyes as I didn't need to read anything and there didn't seem to be any point in looking at the congregation. I thought I'd just about finished. I was flagging, my mouth gumming up. Anything else I had to say about Brendan would remain unspoken. It was our private business. I did still resent him: for his selfishness, his inability to change, his lack of empathy. All my strengths he saw as weaknesses. Surely it hadn't always been like that. But it was like that now because he was dead. He'd had the last word, even though I was speaking at his funeral. And I knew I'd miss him, and he knew I'd miss him because I loved him. And because he was my friend, and I didn't have many friends.

It suddenly occurred to me I'd been standing in the pulpit saying nothing for some time, but I wasn't certain how long it had been. I felt the priest's hand on my shoulder, he was on tiptoe and leaning into the steps, and I opened my eyes. They were all there, numbed and grey and slope-shouldered, row after row of drawn bone masks.

There was a sudden banging, something kicking against wood, agitated and sustained, urgent.

Brendan.

His stupid foot. His nervous agitation. It had sundered the veil. He was kicking himself into life like an in-utero foetus. I always knew he was too stubborn to die. Death by misadventure? He wouldn't allow for it. As always, he was right all along, he'd just nipped into the afterlife for a couple of hours, put St Peter right on a few minor epistemological issues, and now he was back to lord it over the rest of us. Perhaps there were no bars in heaven, so now he was home, kicking up a fuss and kicking shit out of his coffin. Bang, bang, bang.

At the back of the room an usher slipped silently from a pew, and approached the great oak doors of the church. The entire congregation turned to see Scott, sheepishly returning to his seat, his telephone still in his hand. I expect the signal in the church hadn't been too good. He mouthed "Sorry" at me. I looked at Brendan. He was perfectly still.

Outside the church, standing on gravel, I wished I still smoked. I had my hands deep in my trouser pockets and avoided the rest of the congregation. I wondered what the etiquette was. How long did I have to hang around before I could legitimately leave? Other people were leaving already, striding towards their cars, bent into umbrellas. But I had a featured role at the funeral. I'd done a speech, so I reckoned I had to stick around.

Conal approached me. His hands were also in his pockets and his short hair was plastered to his scalp with the rain. His shoulders hunched and the purple eye-bags were more defined still, his skin pale as soap, his blue eyes unblinking. He looked as if he wanted to kill me. The speech had started badly, and I couldn't remember the ending, but it surely didn't warrant violence. But now I was going to die at Brendan's funeral. It was, at least, what he would have wanted.

"Paul." he said, his hand flew from his pocket, and I flinched. He was offering me a cigarette. I took it greedily and he lit it with a gold Zippo in a single fluid movement. Conal had some blurry green dots on the back of his hand, and I was reminded of some of the stories Brendan had told me about his big brother. Conal lit a cigarette of his own and drew on it fiercely, his lips a narrow blue slit. My own cigarette was making me feel both light-headed and queasy, but I continued to smoke.

"That was some speech," he said, at length.

"Yeah, well, you know. Spur of the moment job."

"I think you mentioned a barmaid's tits at some point."

"Did I? Did I?"

He gave me his hand. I shook it weakly.

"It was good. You didn't soft soap it, you know? He could be a bit of a prick, Brendy. You didn't shy away from it. We all knew him. We knew what he was like. You done good. The family appreciate it."

"Thank you," I said, "he was my best friend. He was hard work but I'm going to miss him. I'm really going to miss him."

"You did good. I can see why he called you 'the writer'. Top words. You anything published?"

"Not really."

"That's alright. I don't read books."

"Right."

We had a swift, manly hug in the rain. He nodded at me and crunched off over the wet gravel. I threw my half-finished cigarette to the ground and buried it with the toe of my shoe. Brendan was dead and I'd helped bury him. I'd lowered the coffin into the earth. There was no coming back. Part of my life had gone forever, the rituals abandoned. All the complexities of my social life had been flattened. My life would be boringly simple now, utterly free of incident. Brendan had been the last remnant of my wild and distant youth, a lord of misrule, an insensible man. And I'd lowered him into the greedy earth. It would take him and redistribute him, share him with the teeming morbidities beneath.

There were going to be a lot of fucked up worms.

BATH NIGHT

I WAS WATCHING the film *Les Diaboliques*, when something splashed into my glass of wine. *Les Diaboliques* is the story of two teachers at a provincial French boy's school. One of them is the headmaster's wife, the other his mistress. He mistreats both, so they plot to kill him. They do this by getting him drunk and drowning him in the bath. They then dump him in the school's murky and abandoned swimming pool. Mysterious things start to happen around the school. The reappearance of the damp Prince of Wales check suit he'd been wearing when he was murdered. A small boy says he has seen and spoken to the dead man. The film is filled with unease and disquiet, and the women's guilt is a tangible presence. The ghost is clammily implacable, chasing them down, slow wet footprints on flagstone floors. The women look on helplessly as a boy dives into the swimming pool where the body of the headmaster is hidden. Their fingers claw at their faces, their eyes bulge in horror and, just as the boy's body hits the water, something splashes in my wine glass and I recoil, spilling Shiraz all over my Pixies t-shirt. It was an original *Surfer Rosa* one too—ruined. Another drop of water lands on my thigh, and then another, the grouping is quietly precise, separated by seconds.

I looked up. Water was dripping from my light fittings. It worked its way down the flex like a shiver down a spine and collected into quick, fat tears under the parabola of the lightbulb.

They continued to fall, quick and warm onto my leg. Around the light fitting the ceiling bruised softly. What the fuck was going on?

It must be the woman upstairs. What was she playing at?

I ventured out into the shared hall, slipping on the landfill of takeaway menus that had accumulated on the door mat. I peered up at her darkened door.

"Hello?"

The banister was loose and wobbled like a milk tooth in its socket. The air was heavy with dust, the walls thick with shadow. The hall-light didn't work. It hadn't worked for over a year, but I never bothered to change it because I lived downstairs and never needed it. She must have had to climb those steps in darkness every day. Why hadn't she replaced the lightbulb? I reached the top of the stairs and gave a tentative knock.

"Hello?"

Nothing. What was her name? It was in the Christmas card. Julie? Julia? One of those. I tried both. No response.

What to do? Knocking and saying hello hadn't worked. What should I do now? I did the same things again, and when that didn't work, I tried once again, raising my voice slightly. Then I went downstairs.

It's probably fine, I thought. She's probably fine. It was raining in my living room. Extremely localised rainfall was drenching my sofa. The stain on the ceiling widened and darkened. I went to switch the light off, then thought better of it in case I got electrocuted. I didn't know much about electricity, but I knew it didn't mix well with water.

This was bad. Should I call the police? I didn't want to end up with someone else's bath in my living room, especially if that someone was still in it. I saw visions of her rising fish-eyed and dripping from the tub, and pointing a damp, accusatory finger at me. What had I done? I didn't send her a Christmas card back. That's the only thing she could hold against me. I didn't deserve to be haunted from a watery grave for that. It was a minor social gaffe. I went back into the hall.

"Hello?" I bellowed. "Hello, Julie? Are you okay? IS YOUR TOILET OVERFLOWING?"

I climbed the stair again and pressed my ear to the door. I thought I could hear water flowing, but it might just as easily have been the blood running hot beneath my skin. We gurgle inside.

"Hello, Julia?" Can you hear me? Are you hurt? Are you okay? It's the man from downstairs. I think you might be damaging my property. Not that that's the main issue here if you're hurt. Are you in need of assistance? Are you in need of medical assistance?"

I went downstairs again and flapped up and down the hall. I peeked into my flat and it was still pouring down. I went back into the hall and paced up and down again, until, in a sudden decisive moment, I turned and galloped up the stairs, tripped on the top step in the darkness and body slammed the door, which gave instantly, splintering around the lock like matchwood. I don't know if I intended to break into her flat but, with no time for sight-seeing, I made for the bathroom, stepped over her naked body to reach the bath taps and plunged my arm into the water to remove the plug.

I turned to look at her. There was about an inch of water on the floor, but her face was resting on her left forearm and mouth and nose appeared to be well clear. She was breathing, which was good, but she was also foaming at the mouth which was not. There was a narrow cut on her forehead and pinkish blood in the water that I couldn't account for. She had a toothbrush in her hand, and I realised, with some relief, it accounted for the foaming mouth. I nudged her with my toe.

"Miss? You seem to have had a fall. Miss? Julie? Julia?"

And then I noticed something remarkable. I knew her. We'd met before. She was the girl I hadn't been introduced to at Scott's party a few weeks ago. The drunk girl I'd got on well with, the one who liked cool films. She'd been the upstairs tenant the whole time. How weird was that? Oh, and she was possibly dying in front of me.

I didn't know what to do, so I picked up some towels and started to mop up some of the water. After a few minutes, I realised that she was still naked, so I draped a towel over her. A few minutes after that, I realised that I still hadn't phoned an ambulance, which was probably the first thing I should have done. I dialled 999 and by the time they arrived she was sat up in her dressing gown drinking coffee and feeling mortified. They took her to hospital anyway because of the head injury. She was groggy and didn't recognise me from the party. Which was fine.

What had happened was this: Julia, it was Julia, had been running a bath and decided to brush her teeth. After rinsing her mouth under the tap, she had cracked her head on the corner of the medicine cabinet that was over the sink. This was the source of the mysterious blood in the water. This had left her dazed, and she fell forward smashing her forehead on the edge of the sink. It knocked her out and she fell to the floor, toothbrush in hand, the bath taps continuing to flow until the water spilled over, leaking into my light fittings.

That night, while she was in hospital for observation, I thought about her naked body. I didn't want to, it seemed creepy and intrusive and wrong. I didn't want to sexualise a defenceless, unconscious woman. It was not a sexual scenario when I discovered her body, and I was very busy. There were things to do, and I was just relieved that she was still alive and that the damage to my ceiling was minimal.

But later, as I lay in bed, the soft contours of her naked body flashed into my mind. Her black hair, her white, downy skin, and the moles that peppered her body. Her long eyelashes and longer nose. She had the faint shadow of a moustache and deep hollows beneath her collar bones.

And then I stopped myself, because I was being disgusting. Even in the locked-safe of my head, in the forgotten shell of my bedroom, it was still disgusting. I'd helped her. I'd stepped over her to turn off the taps. I'd checked to see that she was breathing. I'd covered her naked body and called an ambulance. I'd sat with her until the ambulance came. She seemed nice. She was embarrassed, and I was nice to her. I wasn't heroic and I didn't even do things in the right order (check the body and *then* turn off the taps) but I'd done the right thing. And in the city, in this city, that was not nothing. It took slight effort. I'd breached the cell of my own loneliness, and reached out to another human being. I'd more than smashed her door, I'd broken down the isolation of the city. I'd done something for someone else and it hadn't backfired. She could have drowned. She could have destroyed my ceiling, her floor and both of our flats. I'd done the right thing, well and selflessly. Not entirely. I *was* worried about her ruining my room and, initially, I had thought she'd just been pissed, like I say, we share a recycling box. But mainly it had been an attempt to avert disaster. The worst thing I could do now would be to contaminate that fact with masturbatory fantasies. I wanted to have this one thing, this one pure moment where I had acted well, where I had acted at all.

I closed my eyes and saw her naked, white body lying there. And in my mind, I placed a towel over her again. And I rolled over and I fell asleep, the sleep, finally, of the just.

In the morning, before she returned from the hospital, I went out and bought her some flowers and a pretty good bottle of wine. I left them outside her flat with a card that read "Dear Julia, hope you're okay. Have another headache on me!! Best, Paul (downstairs)" I worried about the two exclamation points but thought they might make me seem "fun". When I got in from work that evening, I found a card on the floor. It was a handwritten builder's estimate for her new door.

I sat down on the arm of the sofa, still wearing my coat. My head sank into my chest. I dropped the note to the floor. Of course Julia was billing me for a new door. Of course she was. Why would I expect anything else? I'd just pay it. What else could I do? I should probably thank her. It was a final confirmation of how the world worked. In a way every event in my life had been leading to this point. It was the quiet and devastating culmination of my existence, the last piece in the puzzle, and I could finally see the big picture: a boot kicking a human arse—forever. My arse, toe-punted into eternity.

I was too depressed to move, staring at my feet. There was a drawing on the back of the estimate. It looked to be in the same style as the hand-drawn Christmas card I'd received from her. I picked it up. It was a portrait of a woman lying on the floor with crosses for eyes, her bare arse in the air, and a towel draped over her. Next to her, perched on the edge of a bath, was a drawing of me. I was wearing a breastplate and helmet and there was a halo around my head. It bore the legend: "My Hero". Underneath she'd written: "Sorry about the over-leaf, my idea of a joke. Still a bit funny in the head! Thank you so much for everything. Love Julia (upstairs!) x"

Oh, I thought.

Oh.

These Walls, Thy Sphere

I WAS SITTING in a booth in the Arts Centre. It was an oppressive building, largely comprised of cement blocks and metal railings. The café and bar area were a sort of dingy burnt orange and lit, like everywhere these days, by bare forty-watt bulbs hanging from the ceiling on dangling wires. Lampshades and being able to see properly were *so* last century.

Posters for forthcoming attractions slumped in box-frames on the walls and, at the box office, a girl in a company sweatshirt was over-laughing at everything a goth boy was saying. He was wearing a backpack with a bottle of water attached to it and carrying an umbrella. Obviously an all-terrain goth. I didn't *know* that she was laughing too much, perhaps he was an incredibly funny goth. He didn't look funny, unless she was just laughing at his appearance, in which case he stood there and took it for far too long.

The building was like a brutalist school assembly-hall, and had the high, clattering ambience of a swimming pool. What it really reminded me of was Slade Prison from the sitcom *Porridge*: the bare concrete walls, the central reservation, the clanking metal, though the clanking here was the sound of baristas opening drawers of coffee grounds, and not lags banging tin mugs on cell grills. I used to think that prison looked okay: all telly watching, Page Three lovelies on the walls and peeling oranges. I went to a seventies comprehensive that was infinitely more terrifying than penal servitude. At school I was a lonely Godber without an avuncular Fletch to keep an eye out for me. Not even the teachers bothered. Some of them joined in.

My booth was a large dark-wood cubicle with felt padded benches on either side. It looked as though it should have been soundproof, but this was a Saturday afternoon, and the arts centre was practically a crèche. Progressive looking parents were drinking wine in the afternoon, while their tousle-haired offspring ran wild, skidding about the stone floor and throwing tantrums, bless them. My latte came in a glass without a handle and two lumps of artisan sugar resting on the saucer like pumice stones next to the bath.

I was there to see Powell and Pressburger's *A Canterbury Tale*, a very rare big-screen showing of one of my favourite films. The re-evaluation of the past seems to be generational. We tend to reappraise culture in twenty-year increments, or at least we used to. When I was in my twenties in the late eighties, all the music was based on the sixties. All those chiming Rickenbackers and fringed leather jackets, all those bowl cuts. People from Rippon and Reading wanting to be in Buffalo Springfield. In the nineties flares and wah-wah pedals were everywhere, and we all grooved to funk and soul deep-cuts. Afro wigs appeared at parties. Simpler times. I was born in 1967, and have an abiding fondness for British films of the forties and fifties, particularly those of The Archers, Michael Powell and Emeric Pressburger, whom I think are the de facto genii of British cinema.

Their most famous films, *A Matter of Life and Death*, *Black Narcissus* and *The Red Shoes* are rightly lauded. Hallucinatory, indelible, hugely ambitious and vivid, they're as good as anything in cinema. But I prefer their quieter, stranger black and white films, like *I Know Where I am Going*, an odd, mystical parable set on a non-existent Scottish Island, or this one, *A Canterbury Tale*, which is ostensibly a war propaganda film, but features the following peculiar plot: three strangers, a land girl, a British soldier and an American G.I. are stranded in the titular Cathedral town, and while stuck there decide to solve the mystery of the Glue Man, a phantom presence who spatters local girl's hair with a sticky substance under cover of darkness. It's a real film—I haven't just made that up. They do uncover the culprit—local magistrate, Culpepper, who has been attempting to keep the girls at home so he can show his slideshows on the wonders of English heritage to a captive audience of young men, in the hope that his love for the magic and mystery of Blighty will be passed on to the next generation.

It's a film that makes you ask—who was this film intended for? And what did people make of it at the time? Did the war office think it was money well spent? Did they realise the sexual symbolism, laid on thick, in those supposedly more innocent times? Sometimes glue is just glue.

It might be my favourite film, but I'm aware of the wilful oddness of some of my favourite films. I don't like commercial cinema on principle, but equally I'm not willing to accept the canon of respectable classics. Why should I listen to the nodding greybeards of academia, with their peer-reviewed short-lists of sanctified cinema? Fuck 'em. If you say you like something then I don't like it, because who are you to be telling me anything? You don't even know me.

This leaves me with the oddball stuff, all the unloved and overlooked remnants of forgotten cinema, or the hidden gems as I prefer to call them. And *A Canterbury Tale* is among their number. The bizarre sequence with Esmund Knight's stuttering village idiot, filmed entirely in silhouette, would lend it oddball status alone. Knight, a blind actor, has three roles in this film, none of them blind. How's that for progressive cinema?

I'm not seeing the film on my own. I have a date. Someone wanted to come to the cinema with me. It's Julia from upstairs. She's not here yet. The incident with her concussion and the splintered door, broke the ice rather than traumatising her. I'd asked her out in the shared hallway. She was halfway up the stairs by the time I'd made it out into the hall.

"Hello," I said.

"Hello. You alright?" There was a Tesco bag for life in her hand. The top of a wine bottle nosed out of it.

"Do you want to go and see a film? A specific film. With me."

"What film?" she said, hiding the bag behind her legs.

"It's an old black-and-white English film. It's about a mad bloke who pours glue into girl's hair in the dark."

"Really?"

"That makes it sound shit. Sorry. It isn't shit."

"Oh, okay then," she said, "as long as it isn't shit."

"Really? Great. It really isn't shit. It's great."

I went back into my flat, elated. I heard the door click behind me. I immediately opened the door again and went back out into the hall. Julia was still standing on the stairs.

"When?" she said.

"Thursday evening? Is that okay?"

"What time and where?"

"7.30. The Arts Centre."

"Okay."

"Right."

"Bye."

"Bye. I'll walk you home afterwards," I said.

"Hah," She said.

"Right," I said.

"Just don't put sticky stuff in my hair," she said.

"God, no!"

She turned quickly and went into her flat, and I returned to mine. From upstairs I could hear dislocated cries. I could hear the skirting board being kicked. I smiled.

"Hiyah," said Julia, as she swept into the booth, bringing with her the smell of cold fresh air. She was wearing recently applied lipstick. It hovered over her lips, not quite part of her yet. I realised this was the first time that I'd ever met her when one or other of us wasn't drunk or unconscious, and I rose to greet her with an awkward continental kiss. She smelled good, a rich, incense smell. Smoky, but not cigarettes, though she looked like a smoker.

She'd come straight from work, but she does some arts stuff, so you'd never know. She was wearing a red pleather mini-skirt and a black rollneck. You wouldn't get that in my office.

And she was beautiful. I thought she was beautiful. She had a big nose and big eyes, and she was in her forties, and she looked her age. Her hair was suspiciously blue-black, like Superman's. But, my God, she was beautiful. Her face was eager, her eyes alive. She was looking at me and part of me wanted to hide, but the greater part, finally, wanted to drink it all in, the long draft of the thirsty man. She was saying something, and I was smiling and nodding and then I was saying something, and she was laughing and her laugh was loud and honking, and the most wonderful sound in the world. I asked her if she wanted a drink, and she said red wine and soon the lipstick was on the rim of the glass and the wine had stained the corners of her mouth, and we were talking, and she was so cool. She'd heard of *everyone*—it was like talking to a mate except enjoyable, a mate who actually seemed to like you.

I tried to order another round but she insisted it would be cheaper to get a bottle, then 7.30 came and went and we forgot all about the Glue Man and Canterbury Cathedral because we were talking and talking and we didn't want to break the spell, but eventually she had to excuse herself and clip-clopped off across the cement floor to the toilet, and I sat back against the plush of the booth and smiled because I was having a great time on a date and I couldn't remember this ever happening before. I was relaxed, I was funny and so was Julia. We were laughing a lot. And making a lot of eye contact. I was recognising a lot of sexually specific tics that I gleaned from the Desmond Morris book I'd read. It was going really, ridiculously well.

"Where's my fucking bag?"

The Arts Centre was quiet: everyone was watching the film. There was just the boy behind the bar and the girl at the box office, and now, suddenly, a skinny woman with long dark hair who was shouting at me.

"Where's my bag, you fat cunt?"

I looked around.

"Me?" I said.

"Yes, fucking you," she said, "thief."

"I have no idea what you're talking about." I looked over at Julia's bag. "That bag isn't mine. It's my date's bag."

"I don't give a shit about that . . . tat. Where's my bag?"

And then it suddenly hit me. She was the girl, the girl who'd sat opposite me in the café all those months ago, a year ago, the girl with the big leather bag, the girl with the big leather bag that was stolen.

"I remember you," I said. "You've got it all wrong—I was trying to help you."

"You were trying to help me by stealing all my shit?"

At this point Julia returned from the toilet.

"What's going on?" she said.

"Your boyfriend stole my bag," said the girl.

"He's not my boyfriend," said Julia.

A bit crushing.

"I've only been gone five minutes. He doesn't even have a bag," said Julia.

"This was last year," I said.

Julia looked at me seriously. She was dating a bag-snatcher.

"What happened was, another girl came along and took the bag. I tried to defend the bag but they didn't believe me."

"Who didn't believe you?" said Julia.

"The barista," I said, "I knew I was right. I knew that she was a different girl. She looked a bit like you, but I was right. I tried to defend the bag, but they chucked me out of the café. You were ages. Why were you so long?"

"None of your business," said the girl.

"No, *where* were you?" said Julia, "if you're going to accuse him of stealing, we better have all the facts. Why were you so long?"

"I had diarrhoea," said the girl, "okay? I had really bad diarrhoea."

The boy behind the bar barked a laugh.

"I didn't steal your bag," I said. "A girl came."

"Bullshit. Right, I'm calling the police . . ." She pulled her telephone out of her back-pocket and began to dial. I saw Julia sneaking away, picking up her coat and bag, and I couldn't blame her. The date had been going brilliantly, but now she was sneaking out the back door having had a lucky escape, and I was going to be arrested for a crime I didn't commit like the A Team.

Fine.

Her coat and bag in one hand, Julia reached around the girl and lifted her glass of wine throwing it into the girl's face. She screamed and dropped her phone on the cement floor. White lines snaked across the screen, ice cracking in whisky.

"Run!" Julia yelled, and I grabbed my coat and the pair of us clattered across the Art Centre's floor, past the sliding doors and out into the freedom of the night. We continued to run for another hundred yards, which was about my limit, and I bent double over a concrete bollard, my breath wreathed about me thick as vape, while Julia kept lookout. She looked nervy, but it was clear that the girl had'nt followed us. Julia extended a hand, and I took it gladly.

"Come on, Gangster Number One," she said, "I'll walk you home."

"I *really* didn't steal that bag," I said. "It happened exactly like I said it did: she disappeared, another girl took her bag, and nobody believed me. I'm an innocent man."

"Shame," she said, "I was looking forward to being Bonnie to your Clyde."

"I apologise for not being dangerous and sexy," I said.

"I meant Clyde the orangutan from *Every Which Way but Loose*. Besides, you're no use to me dangerous. Sexy, on the other hand . . ."

She drew me towards her, and we kissed, bathed in the warm amber glow of a pub window. I'm not sure how long we were there, wrapped around each other, deaf to the catcalls of the glazed, grinning faces of the pub patrons drumming on the glass. The kiss broke, and we stared into each other's eyes to a chorus of "Get in there my son".

"Is it always like this?" she asked, "your life? Is it just a series of ridiculous events?"

"It's always like this," I answered.

"Good," she said. "Let's go home. I need to get my own back."

"What do you mean?"

"Well, you've seen *me* naked . . ."

We drifted off into the evening, my arm around her, melting into the shadows only to be found by another lamp further down the street, smaller, neater and closer together each time, until eventually we were an indivisible whole, tight and small and blinking in and out of existence.

FINE

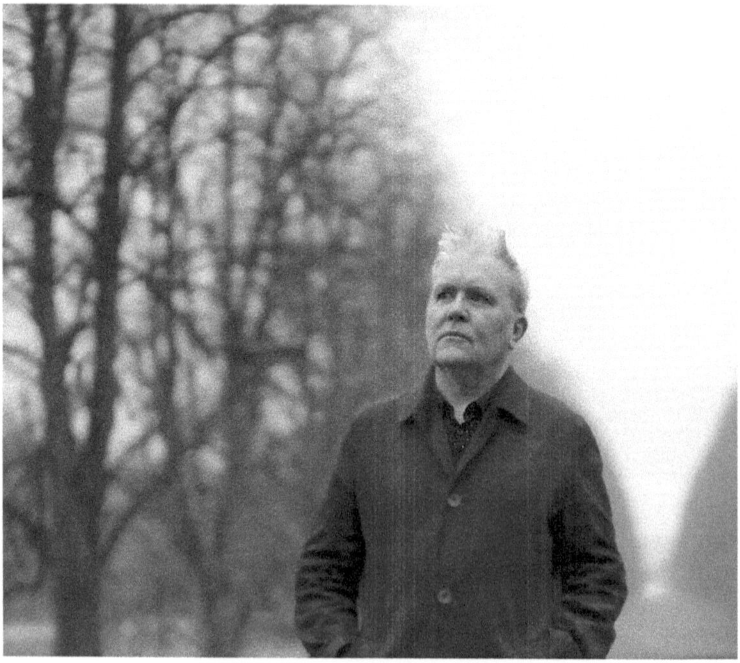

John Patrick Higgins is a writer and director. He lives in Belfast, where it rains.